"There's an old inn le[gend...]"

She glanced at Josh in his heavy coat and boots as he stood in the inn's yard, white snow surrounding him. He was focused intently on her. "If two people kiss in the heart-shaped shadow the rising full moon creates on this tree, they will fall in love with each other for the rest of their lives."

"Have you ever kissed in the shadow?" a deep voice asked beside her.

She turned to peek at Josh, thankful for the darkness that hid the blush warming her cheeks. "No, I haven't. There—look, Josh, I think the shadow is forming," she whispered, watching the shifting dark patterns on the dazzling white snow.

"We can't waste that," Josh said, taking her hand and hurrying down the steps.

"Josh, we can't—"

He rushed her over to stand in the heart-shaped shadow. "It's only a kiss."

"This is absurd," she said, laughing, her heart pounding wildly. "Suppose it comes true? We don't even know each other. You're tempting fate."

He smiled at her, then pulled her to him.

* * *

Kissed by a Rancher is part of *USA TODAY* bestselling author Sara Orwig's Lone Star Legends series.

Dear Reader,

Why do opposites attract and marry each other? I have spent my married life trying to figure this out because that is what I did. I don't have an answer yet, except that life is interesting and you understand *cooperation*.

In *Kissed by a Rancher*, another Texas legend changes the lives of two people who are totally opposite in lifestyles, temperament, backgrounds—in almost everything in their lives except their intense attraction to each other. When Josh Calhoun seeks shelter in a raging blizzard at a small Texas town's bed-and-breakfast, he walks into a world entirely different from his own. Instead of the sophisticated women in his cosmopolitan billionaire rancher's life, he meets the owner, who is a small-town, family-oriented person with definite ideas about what she likes.

Josh Calhoun and Abby Donovan tempt fate by following a Texas legend. From that moment on, their lives are never again the same.

I grew up in a family with a long history of Texas and Tennessee legends. Legends still spark my imagination and were a source for this series, Lone Star Legends. In these stories there are various legends from scary to promises of riches, but this one involves the heart and brings together two unlikely people.

Thank you for your interest in this book.

Sara Orwig

KISSED BY A RANCHER

—

SARA ORWIG

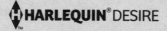
HARLEQUIN® DESIRE

ISBN-13: 978-0-373-73386-6

Kissed by a Rancher

Copyright © 2015 by Sara Orwig

Printed in U.S.A.

www.Harlequin.com

Sara Orwig lives in Oklahoma. She has a patient husband who will take her on research trips anywhere, from big cities to old forts. She is an avid collector of Western history books. With a master's degree in English, Sara has written historical romance, mainstream fiction and contemporary romance. Books are beloved treasures that take Sara to magical worlds, and she loves both reading and writing them.

Books by Sara Orwig

HARLEQUIN DESIRE

Stetsons & CEOs
Texas-Sized Temptation
A Lone Star Love Affair
Wild Western Nights

Lone Star Legacy
Relentless Pursuit
The Reluctant Heiress
Midnight Under the Mistletoe
One Texas Night...
Her Texan to Tame

Lone Star Legends
The Texan's Forbidden Fiancée
A Texan in Her Bed
At the Rancher's Request
Kissed by a Rancher

Visit the Author Profile page at Harlequin.com or saraorwig.com for more titles!

To David and my family with love. Also, with many thanks to Stacy Boyd and Maureen Walters.

One

Josh Calhoun glanced at the red neon sign glowing through the swirling snow. The windows of the Beckett Café were frosted, so he couldn't see if it had closed for the night. As hungry as he was, he was far more interested in finding a bed. Highway patrol troopers had closed the roads, and he couldn't even get back to the tiny airport to sleep on a cold hangar floor or inside his plane. He glanced at the cab's clock: a few minutes past ten. He felt as if it should be around 1:00 a.m.

The taxi left the two blocks of one-story buildings, shops and neon behind as the main street of Beckett, Texas, was swallowed in a white world of howling wind and blowing snow. In spite of the warmth of the cab, Josh shivered. He pulled his jacket collar up while he peered outside at the uninviting storm.

In minutes he spotted a sign swinging in the wind, a spotlight on the ground throwing a strong beam over the announcement of the Donovan Bed and Breakfast Inn. Glumly he stared at the bright red No Vacancy part of the sign.

Even wind-whipped snow could not hide the three-story Victorian-style house that loomed into view. A light glowed over the wraparound porch. Dark shutters flanked the wide windows spilling warm yellow light outside into the stormy night. The driver pulled to the curb.

"Ask for Abby Donovan. She runs the place," the driver said.

"Will do. I'll be right back."

"I'll wait. Abby's a nice person. I don't think she'll turn you out in the cold. You'll see."

Placing a broad-brimmed Stetson on his head, Josh stepped out of the warmth of the cab into the driving wind and streaming snow. Holding his hat against the battering wind, he trudged to the house to ring the bell. Through a window he could see a big living room with people inside and an inviting roaring fire in the fireplace.

When the door swung open, he momentarily forgot why he was there. A slender woman with huge, thickly lashed cornflower-blue eyes faced him. She wore a powder-blue sweater and jeans. He forgot the time, the howling storm and even his plight. Too captivated by eyes that widened and held him, Josh stood immobilized and silent until he realized how he stared at her.

"Abby Donovan?" His voice was husky, and he still was lost in her gaze.

She blinked as if as captured as he had been. "I'm Abby."

"I'm Josh Calhoun. I flew in to see someone about buying a horse, and then I couldn't get back to the airport. I was told to see you about a place to stay. I know you have a No Vacancy sign out, but at this point, I'm willing to sleep on the floor just to get in out of this blizzard."

"I'm so sorry, but we're overbooked. I already have people sleeping on the floor."

"My cabdriver can't get back to the airport. They've closed the roads."

"I'm sorry, but even the overflow space is taken here. I've let two people come in tonight who will sleep on sofas, and we have two on pallets on the floor. That's the most I can possibly accommodate. I have eighteen adults in rooms, plus nine children. Four other people live here at least part of the time. I don't have extra blankets or pillows now—"

"I stopped and bought blankets and a pillow at the only store open in this town just as they closed. I'm desperate."

"Oh, my," she said, staring at him with a slight frown. Her rosy lips were full, enticing. He tried to focus on getting a bed for the night and stop thinking about the possibility of kissing her. He couldn't recall ever having this type of reaction to a total stranger, much less under his present circumstances. His gaze roamed over her, and he was even more surprised by his attraction to her, because her sandy-blond hair was caught up behind her head in a ponytail, giving her a plain look that shouldn't have done anything to his pulse. All he had to do was gaze into her eyes, though, and a physical response strummed in him. Her riveting blue eyes were unique.

"Abby, I'm desperate. I have bedding. I can sit in a chair. My cabdriver has little kids and wants to get home to them. Just any corner will do. Even a kitchen floor, and I'll get out of your way in the morning. I'll pay you double what you charge for a room."

Her frown deepened. "Come in while we talk. The air is cold."

"Yes, it is," he said as he stepped inside a wide hallway dominated by winding stairs to the second floor. Warmth enveloped him, and his spirits lifted a fraction. A floor mat was close, and he stamped his booted feet. "I can provide payment in advance, an extra fee— whatever you would like. I can't tell you how much I would appreciate this. I really am desperate. I was up until three last night working on a business deal in Arizona and flew in here today on the way home to see about the horse. I didn't have dinner. I'm tired and cold. I can't get home. It's a miserable night and even more miserable without a place to stay. What can I do to help if I stay here? Order in breakfast for everyone?"

Shaking her head, her frown vanished. "There's nowhere in Beckett you could order breakfast. I cook, and it'll be better than trying to order in at this time of night or in the morning. If this snow doesn't stop, no restaurants will be open."

"I'm sure you're right. You're highly praised in town, and I also heard you're softhearted, generous, kind—"

"Stop," she said, a faint smile appearing. "Tell me more about yourself. We're going to be in close quarters, more so than if you just called at an ordinary time and checked in for a room."

Josh was amused by being asked to give a reference, because he was well-known in Texas. "I'm Josh Calhoun from Verity, Texas, and I own a business, Calhoun Hotels."

Her gaze swept over him from his wide-brimmed

Stetson to his hand-tooled boots. "You're buying a horse, but you're in the hotel business?"

"I'm a rancher, too. The hotel headquarters are in Dallas, where I have another home, so you can check that out easily by calling the hotel's front desk. The sheriff of Verity can tell you about me because we've known each other all our lives," Josh said as he withdrew his wallet and flipped it open to show her his driver's license and fishing license. He was turning to the next license when she placed her fingers over his.

The contact sizzled, startling him and causing him to look up. She had stepped closer, and he could detect an old-fashioned lilac perfume. Again, he was caught and held by her stare.

She shook her head slightly. "You don't have to show more identification," she said, stepping away. "All right, you can stay tonight. You can sleep on the sofa in my suite, but I will not share my bathroom, so you'll have to go across the hall to a central one."

"That sounds like paradise," he said, smiling at her. "Thanks, Abby. This means a lot to me, because it's a deplorable night." He wondered if he could talk her into going to dinner with him some night. The cold and relief of acquiring a room must have affected his judgment, because she definitely didn't look like his type of woman. He didn't know her, either, and he didn't ask strangers to go out with him. "I'll get my bedding and pay the cabbie. I'll be back in a minute."

"The front door will be unlocked. I'll lock it after you're back inside."

He stepped closer to her. "You're not going to regret this."

She blinked as if startled. "I certainly hope I don't," she replied breathlessly.

He turned and left, pulling the door closed behind him. Holding his hat squarely on his head again, he sprinted to the taxi and climbed inside. "I got the room. Thanks for the ride," he said, drawing bills out of his wallet. "Thanks for getting me back into town after seeing about the horse. And thanks for your encouragement and for stopping so I could buy a pillow and blanket."

"Glad you found a place. Sorry I couldn't help more, but with the kids plus my in-laws staying, my two-bedroom duplex is not the best place, although you could have come if nothing else had turned up. Good luck to you. When the roads open and you're ready to go back to the airport, call—you have my card. I'll come get you."

"Thanks, Benny," Josh said, glancing at the man's identification card attached to the visor, knowing he would have stayed anywhere he could find before imposing on the cabbie and his family with four little ones plus in-laws in a tiny place. "I won't forget all you've done." Josh tucked an extra-large tip in with the other bills he gave the cabdriver.

"Mister, you made a mistake," the driver said, seeing how much money he had in his hand.

"No, I didn't. That's a thank-you. Take care of yourself and your family," Josh said.

The man smiled. "Thanks. That's a generous tip."

Josh started to step outside but stopped and looked back. "Does Ms. Donovan have a husband who helps her run the inn?"

"No. She's single—from a big family. Her grandmother used to run the place. Now Abby does, and Grandma Donovan lives up on the top floor with some other elderly relatives or over at her daughter's house, which is next door."

"I see," Josh said, deciding the town was small enough that everyone knew everyone else. "Thanks again." He stepped out into the snow to dash back to the inn.

Abby appeared instantly to lock the front door and switch off the porch light. Wind whistled and howled around the house.

"I'll show you where to put your things," she said, walking down the hall and turning as it branched off. "This is my suite." She stepped into a room and turned on a ceiling light. The room had a polished oak floor with a hand-woven area rug, antique mahogany furniture and bookshelves filled with books and family pictures. Green plants gave it an old-fashioned, cozy appearance that made him think of his grandparents' house. A stone fireplace had a smoldering fire with a screen in front of it.

"I started the fire a while ago so my room would be warm after I told everyone good-night," she said. "Most of the guests are in the big living room, and they go to their own rooms about eleven, when I shut everything down. Tonight is a little different because no one can get up and leave in the morning, so I think some will watch a movie. Suit yourself about what you do. You can leave your things and join us, or if you prefer, you can stay in here. There is a door from my bedroom into the hall, so I can come and go that way and not disturb you. You'll have this room to yourself. As soon as I get towels for you and get you registered, I'll go join them again."

"I'll go with you," he said, placing his pillow and blanket on the sofa before shedding his coat. He wore a thick brown sweater over a white dress shirt, jeans and boots and was glad he had dressed warmly.

"You'll be too long for that old-fashioned sofa. Would you rather sleep on the floor?"

"I'll be fine. Just to have a roof over my head is paradise. I don't mind my feet hanging off the sofa," he said, smiling at her. Once again he received a riveting look that momentarily immobilized him until she turned away.

"I'll get your towels," she said and left. He watched her cross the hall and disappear into a room. She returned to hand him clean towels and washcloths.

"If you'll come with me, you can register."

Josh followed her to the front desk of polished dark wood with scratches from what must have been years of use. He glanced around at the decorative staircase rails. "This place looks Victorian."

"It is. It's been in my family for five generations now." She turned a ledger toward him. "Please sign your name. I'll need a credit card. Since you'll be on the sofa, I'll just charge you a discounted rate. Here are the rates and details about staying here," she added, handing a paper to him. "And here's a map of the inn and a map of the town of Beckett, although you won't be leaving tomorrow, because we're supposed to get a lot more snow and possibly sleet."

"No, I'm stuck probably through tomorrow at least."

"Everything has shut down—highways, roads and businesses will be closed tomorrow. They've already had the announcements on television and said schools will be closed Monday." She reached under the desk and produced a small flashlight. "We heard on the radio that half the town is without power because of ice on electric lines. I'm giving all the guests flashlights. This is an old house, and candles are dangerous."

"Thanks." Pocketing the flashlight, Josh barely

glanced at the papers she handed him as he studied her instead. Her smooth, flawless skin and rosy cheeks added to her appeal. What was it about her that fueled this tingling awareness of her? It wasn't her personality, because he barely knew her and had spoken with her only briefly. Her fuzzy sweater came to her thighs and hid her figure, so that wasn't the electrifying draw. She was a nice person who was being helpful. That should be all. Instead, he had a scalding awareness of her that made him think about asking her out, fantasize about dancing with her and holding her, and wonder what it would be like to kiss her and make love with her. She was providing shelter and comfort; maybe it was his long hours of work over the past few days and now the storm that caused his reaction to her. He had slept little for over a week.

When she turned the register around, she read what he had signed. "This gives a Dallas address. Do you consider Dallas home instead of Verity?"

"I live and work in Dallas most of the time. I also have a ranch in west Texas. The closest town is Verity," he replied. She nodded as she gathered more papers to hand to him.

"So you're a hobby rancher," she said.

"Yes, at least for now. Someday I'll move to the ranch and do that full-time and let someone else run the hotel business for me. I go to the ranch when I get a chance, but that rarely happens," he admitted, thinking there weren't many people who knew he missed ranching and wondering why he was telling a stranger.

"Here's the schedule for tomorrow," she said. "Normally breakfast runs from seven-thirty until 9:00 a.m. Since no one can get out tomorrow, we'll start at 8:00 a.m. and go until nine-thirty."

"Thanks. The breakfast time is fine."

"I'll be going back to join the others now unless you have anything else you want to ask me about," she said, looking up, those wide eyes capturing his full attention again.

"Thanks, no. I'll follow you."

"We've been singing. I play the piano or leave it to a guest."

They entered a large living room that ran almost the length of the east side of the house and was furnished in early American maple with a hardwood floor and area rugs. A fire burned low in the fireplace, adding to the inviting appeal of the room. Two small children slept in adults' arms. Five children sprawled on the floor or in an adult's lap. A couple of men stood to offer Abby a seat. Smiling, she thanked them and asked the men to sit.

"We've been waiting. Let's sing some more," someone said.

"Folks, this is another guest—Josh Calhoun of Dallas, Texas," Abby said, smiling and glancing at him while he acknowledged her introduction with a nod and wave of his hand.

People said hi as Abby crossed the room to slide onto the piano bench. She played a song Josh had heard his grandmother play, a song from his childhood that he was surprised to discover he still knew when he joined in the singing.

As they sang, he watched her play. She was not his type in any manner, other than being a woman. He couldn't understand his reaction to her. She was plain, with her hair in an unflattering thick ponytail, and she wore no makeup. She ran a bed-and-breakfast inn in a small west Texas town. He would never ask her out.

He looked out the window at the howling storm blowing heavy snow in horizontal waves. Snowflakes struck the warmer storm window, melted slightly, slid to the bottom and built up along the frame. It was a cozy winter scene, but he wished he were flying home tonight.

Relaxing, he leaned back in the chair and sang with the others while he reflected that he hadn't experienced an evening like this in years. He felt as if he had stepped back to a different time and way of life, and he began to relax and enjoy himself.

After another half hour, Abby turned and slid off the piano bench to take a bow. "That should do for tonight's songfest. Does anyone want hot chocolate? If so, I'll be glad to make some. The entertainment room is open, and Mr. Julius said he will be in charge of the movie. Right now, for hot cocoa, just come to the kitchen."

She left the room. People followed her out until Josh was the only one left. He turned off all the lights except one. He sat again, stretching out his legs and leaning back to gaze at the snow. A few red embers of the dying fire glowed brightly in gray ashes.

He heard tapping and looked again at the window. Sleet struck the glass, building up swiftly on top of the snow at the bottom. He placed his hands behind his head. He couldn't go anywhere or do anything for the rest of the night and probably all day tomorrow. As a peaceful contentment filled him, he thought that an unplanned holiday had befallen him, and he intended to enjoy it.

"You don't want any hot chocolate?"

He glanced around to see Abby entering the room. As he stood, she motioned to him to be seated. "No, thanks," he said. "I'm enjoying the quiet and the storm now that I'm inside and it's outside. I'm beginning to think I'm getting a much-needed vacation."

"That's a good way to look at being stranded. I usually let the fire burn out this time of night. Did you plan to sit here a lot longer?" she asked.

"I'm fine. Let the fire die. I'll turn out the light when I go. If you aren't going to watch the movie, sit and join me," he said.

"Thanks. I will while I can. Mr. Julius knows how to deal with the movie."

"My cabdriver said you're single. This is a big place to run by yourself."

"I'm definitely not by myself," she said, smiling as she sat in a rocker. "I have a long list of people I can rely on for help. I have a brother and a sister nearby, and my grandmother lives here part of the time. I can turn to her for advice if I need it because she used to own and run this place."

"So there are three kids in your family?"

"Right. I'm the oldest. The next is my brother, twenty-year-old Justin, in his second year at a nearby junior college on an academic scholarship. He helps with the bed-and-breakfast and lives at home with Mom. Arden, the youngest at seventeen, is a junior in high school, and she also works here at the inn and lives at home. What about you?"

"I've got two brothers and one sister. This is a big bed-and-breakfast—I'm surprised it doesn't hold more people than you listed earlier."

"I mentioned the people on the third floor who are permanent residents. My grandmother stays here about half of the year. I have two great-aunts who live here part of the year, and I have Mr. Hickman, who is elderly. His family is in Dallas. He's told me that his mar-

ried sons run a business he had. They have asked him
to move to Dallas and live with them, but he grew up
here and came back here when he retired and his wife
was still living. I think she's the one who wanted to return to Beckett because she still had relatives here. His
wife was my grandmother's best friend, so he lives here.
He has a little hearing problem, but he's in relatively
good health. There is an elevator the elderly residents
can take, so they don't use the stairs. My aunts and my
grandmother are gone right now—my grandmother at
Mom's and my aunts visiting their families."

"Do you have to take care of them?"

"No, not really. I have a van and drive them to town
once a week, and I'll take them to church. My brother
or sister or I take them for haircuts, little things. They
just need someone around. By living here, they have
that. My great-aunts' families have scattered and are
on both coasts. They don't want to move, but they may
have to someday. Right now, they're happy here with
my grandmother and our part of the family."

"That's commendable of you to let them live here.
You're young to be tied down to a bed-and-breakfast."

"I'm over twenty-one," she said, smiling at him.
"Twenty-five to be exact."

"This is a lot of responsibility," he remarked, noting
that her attire hid her figure, except for the V-neck of
her sweater, which revealed curves. Also, even in suede
boots, it was obvious she had long legs as she stretched
them out and crossed her feet at her ankles.

"It's fun, and I meet interesting people. I can work
here in my hometown, actually work at home."

"For some, working at home in your hometown is a
drawback, not a plus," he said, thinking he didn't know
a single woman like her with such a simple life.

"For me it's a definite plus. I've never been out of Texas and never been out of my hometown much beyond Dallas or north to Wichita Falls or around west Texas, south to San Antonio once. I don't really want to go anywhere else. Everyone I love is here."

Thinking of his own travels, Josh smiled. "You're a homebody."

"Very much of one," she said. "I suspect you're not, and you sound as if you're a busy man. Are you married, Josh?"

"No, I'm single, not into commitment at this point in my life. I travel a lot, and this is a job I like," he said. "Or have liked. At heart I'm a rancher, which is why I came to Beckett to see about a horse."

Big blue eyes studied him, and he thought again how easy it was to look at her.

"You have two vastly different interests—I guess, vocations—ranching and the corporate world," she said. "Does your family live close?"

My siblings are here in Texas, but our parents retired in California. Are both your parents next door?"

"Mom is. She's divorced. She's Nell Donovan, a hairdresser who has a shop in her house. Her story is well-known in town, so it's no secret—my dad ran off with a younger woman he met on his business travels. That was when I was fourteen. He traveled a lot."

"Sorry that he left your mother and your family."

"We hardly saw him anyway because of his job."

"So besides this inn and family, what do you like to do?"

"Gardening, swimming. I'd like to have a pool here, but so far, that hasn't worked out. I like little kids. Once a week I have a story hour at the library and read to preschool kids. I also like movies and tennis."

The thought flitted to mind again to ask her to dinner when the storm was over and the snow melted. Instantly, he vetoed his own thought. She was the earnest type who would take everything seriously. With a sigh, he turned back to look at the fire, trying to forget her sitting so close. It was even more difficult to ignore the tingly awareness of her that he couldn't shake.

"Is there a guy in your life?"

"Sort of," she said, smiling. "There's someone local. We've grown up knowing each other, and we like the same things, so we occasionally go out together. I always figure someday we'll marry, but we seldom talk about it. Neither of us is in a hurry."

"That doesn't sound too serious," Josh said, wondering what kind of man the guy was to have that type of relationship.

She shrugged. "We're after the same things. He wants never to move from Beckett, and I don't either. Our lives are tied up here. He's an accountant, and we're both busy. It's pretty simple."

They lapsed into silence. Josh wondered if in a few months he would even remember her.

"I hope no one else appears on your doorstep and wants shelter," he remarked after a time. "I have two blankets, and I'd feel compelled to give him a blanket and let him sleep on the floor in the room I have."

"I've turned off the porch light, and I can't take anyone else. In the morning I'll have to cook for thirty-five people. We barely have enough of certain food items, and my brother and sister are both out of town, so I'm without help. I can't handle another person."

"I'll help you cook breakfast," Josh volunteered, the words coming without thought.

She laughed softly. "Thanks. You don't look like the type to have done much kitchen work."

He grinned. "I'm a man of many talents," he joked. "I've cooked. I've camped and cooked, cooked as a kid. Occasionally I cook at home, but rarely, I'll admit. I can help. I can serve and that sort of thing."

"Watch out, I'll take you up on your offer."

"I mean it. I'll help you," he said, still wondering why he was so drawn to her. He should have gone to bed an hour ago or when he arrived. "What time will you begin cooking?"

"About six. You don't have to get up that early."

"I'm usually up that early. I'll set the alarm on my phone," he said, getting his phone from his pocket. "I haven't had a call since I arrived," he added, realizing that was a switch in his life, as different as so many other things about this night.

"You surely don't get many calls at night."

"Sometimes. Not getting any is a unique change in my life, and I can live with it tonight easily." He put away his phone. "It's like a holiday. Tell me more about your family."

He settled back in the chair, listening and talking to her as the fire died into gray ashes. It was after one in the morning when she stood. "I should go to bed. Six a.m. will come soon."

He stood to walk with her, stopping at the door to his room for the night. "I'll see you at six. Thanks again for this room."

"Thanks for offering to help in the morning. Good night, Josh."

"Good night," he replied in a husky voice, gazing into her eyes and as riveted as he had been the first moment he had seen her. Still puzzled by his reaction to her, he turned to his door.

Then he glanced down the hall to see her ponytail swing with each step as she walked away. There was nothing about her that should set his heart racing, but it did. He still wanted her in his arms, wanted to kiss her at least, before he left Beckett forever. What made his heart beat even faster were the slight reactions she'd had—her blue eyes widening, a sudden breathless moment in which neither of them spoke—that told him she had felt something, too. He didn't intend to let that go by without doing something to satisfy his curiosity.

Two

Certain Josh stood watching her, Abby felt her back tingle as she walked to her door. What was it about him that made her heartbeat race and took her breath away? She hadn't had that kind of reaction to anyone since she was a teenager. She occasionally dated Lamont Nealey, who lived close by. She had grown up friends with him, closer friends than with any other man, but he never stirred a quicker heartbeat. A slight physical contact with Lamont never made her tingle all over.

As she changed into flannel pajamas, she kept glancing at the door that separated her from Josh. She couldn't shake her awareness of him so close at hand.

She smiled as she thought about his offer of help with breakfast because he had to be wealthy and influential. He probably had a lot of people working for him and keeping him from everyday tasks. She didn't really expect him to pitch in and help.

* * *

The first thing Abby did on waking was slip into her robe and shove her feet into fuzzy slippers to walk to the window. While the wind continued to howl, she opened the drapes and stared at the falling snow. It meant more business, but she never lacked long for business. It was the third weekend in March. A snowstorm rarely occurred so late, but this had been a cold winter in Beckett. With more snow, no one would be leaving the inn, and her brother and sister couldn't get home, so she had a day of work ahead of her.

She glanced at the closed door to the sitting room and wondered how Josh had fared on her short sofa. Her gaze went to the clock, and she hurried to shower.

She spent too long deciding what to wear, finally giving up and pulling on faded jeans, a green sweater and her suede boots. She had told Josh 6:00 a.m. but went to the kitchen half an hour earlier so she could get started alone.

At six on the dot she heard his boots against the wood floor, and her pulse speeded—something she wished wouldn't happen.

"Good morning," Josh said, bringing a dynamic charge into the air as he smiled at her. He had on a navy sweater, jeans and boots and looked like a cowboy in an ad in one of the Western magazines. "Or at least it's a good snowy morning. I see more of the white stuff coming down."

"Sorry. I think you're stuck for a time. Did you get any sleep on the short sofa?"

"Yes, I did. I'm enormously grateful that I didn't have to sleep in the lobby of your town's only hotel."

"I'm sure they would have let you sit in a chair all night."

"They had some employees who couldn't get home, so they were as booked up and as overcrowded as you. I think I was in the town's only available taxi."

"I know you were. We have only one taxi, with people taking different shifts to drive."

He smiled. "What can I do to help? It looks as if you've been up awhile and working. How about I get the pots and pans washed?"

"Wonderful," she said, surprised he would pick such a job. "I'm getting the breakfast casseroles made. The biscuit dough is rising. I'll get the fruit and coffee soon. The table is ready. We're moving along."

"What you mean is, you're moving along. Pretty good for working without any help. You will make someone a good wife," he said, smiling at her as he crossed the kitchen.

"Are you interested?" she teased, certain there was no way he would have any designs on her—or anyone right now—as a wife. He had been about to pass her, but he stopped and turned to look at her. He stood close, and she wished she could take back her flirty remark.

"If I were looking for a wife, I would want to find out what other qualities you have along with capable, kindhearted and fun. Without looking for a wife, it might be interesting to find out," he teased back, his eyes twinkling and making her insides flutter.

"I should have stuck to talking about what work needs to be done," she whispered, wishing she weren't breathless. "I don't usually joke like that with the guests."

"You mean flirt like that with the guests," he said with amusement, and she could feel the blush that swept across her cheeks. Something flickered in the depths of his eyes, and his smile vanished as he looked more intently at her. "Now I really do want to find out," he said in a deeper tone of voice.

"No, you don't. It wouldn't possibly interest you. In every way," she whispered, "I lead a quiet life without excitement, without the outside world intruding, without—" She stopped to stare at him.

"Without what?" he prompted, stepping closer, his gaze searching hers.

"If you wait a lifetime, you won't get an answer from me on that one. It's my fault we're on a subject we don't need to discuss. Let's go back to talking about breakfast."

"That makes what you said all the more interesting," he remarked, placing his hands on both sides of her and hemming her in against the counter, leaning even closer. His eyes were a dark brown, his brown hair straight and neatly combed. His jaw was clean-shaven and she could detect the fresh smell of his aftershave. Her heart pounded, and she couldn't get her breath.

"Josh, maybe I should take care of breakfast alone," she said.

"I disturb you?"

"You've disturbed me since you rang the bell last night at ten," she said bluntly. "I need to get back to breakfast before I burn something."

A faint smile lifted one corner of his mouth. "My morning has started out better than I ever dreamed possible," he said quietly and dropped his hands, moving back.

She passed him, going to the dining room even though she had the table set and ready. She opened a drawer in a buffet and got two serving spoons, moving without thinking about what she was doing, trying to give her pounding heart a chance to slow to normal.

For a moment she had thought he was going to kiss her. With the kind of reaction she had to him, she shouldn't be alone with him. She didn't need distraction from her routine life, or a charmer like Josh, a man who'd merely stopped in Beckett because of a storm. He was another man like her father. The charmer, the traveler, the businessman who could not settle or be faithful. Josh had the same knack for making friends with people he met, and any man with a private jet did a lot of traveling, constantly reminding her of her father. She shivered and turned back to work.

When the weather permitted, Josh would leave, and he would not return. Her heart did not need to get caught up with someone who would go on his way without a thought for Beckett or anyone who lived here.

Returning to the kitchen, she glanced at Josh as he stood at the sink filled with soapy water with his sleeves pushed up, his watch on the windowsill while he scrubbed pans. Amazed that he would work on a tedious, routine job he didn't have to do, she went on to get breakfast, trying to forget Josh or her response when he had stood close or when he flirted.

They worked quietly together, but even as she concentrated on breakfast as the morning progressed, she was aware of Josh working nearby.

Though it was still early for breakfast, she heard shuffling in the hall. As she expected, her tenant Mr. Hickman entered the kitchen, smiling at her. "Good morning, Abby. You look as beautiful as ever."

"Good morning, Mr. Hickman. Thank you. What can I do for you?"

He pulled his brown cardigan closer over his white shirt. "The snow has made me hungry. Can I get a poached egg and a piece of French toast? I don't suppose that's on the menu for this morning."

"I'll fix it for you and you can sit in here to eat. You remember our agreement?"

"Certainly. If I ask for something special, I'll eat it in the kitchen so the others do not expect special favors," he said, chuckling. "I brought yesterday's paper because I don't think we'll get one today."

"I don't think we will, either. Josh, our latest guest, is helping. He can eat in here with you and keep you company," she said, and Josh turned around, drying his hands. "Josh, meet Mr. Hickman. Mr. Hickman, this is Josh Calhoun from Verity and Dallas. He came late last night."

"How do you do, Mr. Hickman," Josh said, shaking the elderly man's hand gently.

"Come join me for breakfast," Mr. Hickman said.

"Mr. Hickman's having a poached egg and French toast," Abby told Josh. "Would you like that, too?"

"I've seen the breakfast casserole and the biscuits— I'd like them if you have enough."

"We have plenty," she said. "I'll get coffee and juice for both of you."

"Go on with what you have to do," Josh said, "and I'll take care of us. If you need help with serving out there, I'll do it."

"Thank you," she replied, surprised again that he was willing to work.

It was after eight and she expected people to begin showing for breakfast, so she hurried to get things ready, poaching the egg and making French toast for Mr. Hickman. She wondered whether Josh minded sitting with him, but in minutes she heard them in conversation and realized Josh seemed happy talking to the elderly man and vice versa. She knew Mr. Hickman was happy, because he spent many long hours without anyone to talk to.

When the first guests came downstairs to be seated for breakfast, she picked up a large serving dish holding the casserole. Josh stepped in front of her, his fingers brushing hers as he took the dish from her. "Let me. You just fill the plates or whatever you do. I'll take things to the dining room. I waited tables in college. I told Mr. Hickman I'd be right back, and he's reading his paper."

"You're nice to sit with him," she said.

"He reminds me of a grandfather I was close to. I like Mr. Hickman."

She felt a pang. She realized she had been hoping Josh would disappoint her and not like eating in the kitchen or with the elderly man, which would cause her to lose some of her attraction for him. Instead, she was more drawn to him in spite of wishing she weren't.

She handed the plates to him and went back to fill more. She wondered about his life, and if he had needed a job waiting tables to make the money to go to school. It had been late last night so she hadn't looked him up on the web, but today she would do a little research on him.

Soon she was too busy dealing with her guests to think about Josh. Finally the dining room was empty and Mr. Hickman had gone to the living room, taking his paper with him.

"Now I'm going to have breakfast," she told Josh, helping herself. "Can I get you something else?"

He stood to pour another cup of coffee. "I'll get what I want. When you sit, I'll join you." He headed to the dining room and returned carrying dishes, which he placed in the sink. When she finally sat down at the table to eat, he picked up his cup of steaming coffee and sat facing her.

"So what did you and Mr. Hickman talk about?"

"He's interesting. He's a fisherman, so we talked about fishing holes and fly-fishing and the biggest trout caught around here, which of course was in a pond that had been stocked."

"So you have time to fish on top of being a business-man and a rancher."

"No, not as often as I'd like. I miss it."

"Maybe this snow is good for you—chance to stop the constant work and enjoy life and that sort of thing," she said.

"Oh, I know how to enjoy life," he said quietly, giving her a look that made his remark personal.

"Relax, Josh. Enjoy this snow. I'd be as lost in your busy corporate world as you are in mine."

"Do you like to dance?"

"I love to dance but do little of it. I don't get out often. If I go out, it's with Lamont Nealey, whom I've known forever the friend I was telling you about last night. When we go out, we go to a movie or something on that order."

"You think I'm missing out on life," Josh said, "and I think you are. At the same time, I think we have a bit of common ground where we view life the same way. You're a family person just as I'm a family person."

"So tell me about your family."

He reached across the table and wrapped his fingers lightly around her wrist with his thumb where he could feel her pulse. "Coward," he accused her softly. "I'll leave it alone now, but we'll take up this subject again sometime soon."

"You didn't see the sign when you came in that reads

'Guests do not flirt with the staff,'" she said, smiling at him.

"I sure as hell didn't see any such sign, and if I had, I would pay no attention to it. Not when I get a response from the staff like the one I'm getting right now," he said, his thumb pressing slightly on her wrist. "Your pulse is galloping."

"That means nothing," she said, too aware of his brown eyes that seemed alert, observant and curious.

"Not where I come from," he retorted. "You want me to tell you what it means?"

"No. You tell me about your family or I'm going to join the guests in the living room."

With a faint smile, Josh sat back in his chair. "I have three siblings," he said. "Two older brothers, Mike and Jake, plus a younger sister, Lindsay."

She listened, learning about his family but still knowing little about his background. From what he had said last night, she suspected a lot of Texans knew who he was. She had an idea he was well-known by wealthy Texas businessmen and probably by Texas socialites.

She was interrupted when a guest came for a late breakfast. As she served it, Josh poured coffee.

Through the morning he worked, doing whatever she needed, and he was a big help to her. Breakfast was over and the kitchen cleaned by a quarter past ten.

"Josh, thanks so much," she said. "Now I'll have a break before lunch, which I'm serving because of the weather. No one can get out for lunch."

"I'm getting the hang of it. I can help with lunch."

That surprised her—or maybe it shouldn't have. "I'm taking a short break. Come back in a little while and we can get started."

"Sure," he said, jamming a hand in his pocket and leaving the kitchen.

As she headed out and walked past the library, Mr. Hickman lowered his paper and motioned to her to come in.

"Perhaps you should close the door," he said, stirring her curiosity about what he wanted. "Do you know who your guest Josh Calhoun is? Or his company?"

"I don't know much about him. He said his business is Calhoun Hotels, and he's a rancher occasionally," she said. "He's just staying until the roads open, and then I'm sure he'll be gone forever."

"Oh, no. I think he'll come back to fish with me."

"I hope so, if that's what you want, but he sounds as if he's wrapped up in his work," she said.

Mr. Hickman's brow furrowed, and his watery blue eyes gazed into the distance. "Perhaps at the moment." His attention returned to her, and he stared at her a moment before he smiled. "He asked a few questions about you. He's a very nice young man. A knowledgeable fisherman, from his conversation. I liked him."

"Well, that's good, because he's here for a few days."

Mr. Hickman whispered, "If I were Josh Calhoun, I would ask you out to dinner."

"I think Josh has a girlfriend," she whispered back, not knowing whether he did or not, but wanting to stop Mr. Hickman from pursuing that topic with Josh or anyone else.

Mr. Hickman nodded. "Nice fella. Too bad."

"Mr. Hickman, you like Lamont. That's who I go out with sometimes."

"If I were Lamont, I would not wait two or three months between dates. I would never have won my Barbara if I had done that."

She smiled and patted his hand. "Lamont is nice, and we're very much alike. That's what counts."

"Lamont is my accountant, and you're my landlady. Frankly, I don't think you're as much alike as you seem to think."

"Do not be a matchmaker, Mr. Hickman. I'm very happy with Lamont. Now I'm going to my room. Are you going upstairs?"

"No, I'll sit and read the rest of yesterday's paper," he said. "You may leave the door open when you go."

Smiling, she left to go to her room, but her smile faded when she glanced at the closed door between her bedroom and her sitting room, where Josh had slept. He was in his room now, just on the other side of the door. What was he doing? She thought about her reassurances to Mr. Hickman regarding how alike she and Lamont were and how happy she was going out with him. She gazed at the door as if looking at Josh instead and thought about how he had flirted and what fun she had had with him this morning—something that was totally lacking in her relationship with Lamont. Lamont was an old friend. There was none of the electricity that sparked between Josh and her, no flirting, no fun in that way.

She hadn't stopped to think about it before. Was she really that happy with Lamont? Would they ever marry or just go through life as friends? What did she really want? She had never questioned her relationship with him.

Always, her thoughts turned to her parents—she never wanted to be hurt the way her mother had been when her father had walked out on them. Shaking her head as if she could get rid of thoughts about Josh, she knew Lamont was the type of man she needed in her

life: steady, reliable, dependable. Those qualities were
what counted and meant a satisfying life.

For an instant, a memory flashed of her father, who
could coax a laugh from her and make the whole world
seem magical. She focused on the inn, trying to avoid
remembering how much she had loved her father. The
hurt still came after all these years any time she recalled
the shock when he'd suddenly left them.

She went to her computer and pulled up Calhoun
Hotels and read about Josh's business, but she found
little actual information about him.

When she returned to the kitchen to start on lunch,
she was surprised to discover Josh already had the table
set and was preparing a pitcher of ice water.

"You're a help. You don't have to keep working.
You're a paying guest, so go do something enjoyable,"
she said.

As he shook his head, he grinned. "I don't mind, and
it keeps me busy. It's a change of pace for me and keeps
my thoughts off what is piling up in my office while
I'm gone." He glanced out the window. "The snow has
finally stopped."

"I checked the weather report before coming down—
we might get more before morning."

"As soon as the roads open, I'll rent a car and drive
home. I can rent a car in Beckett, can't I?"

"Oh, yes. We have car rental at the airport. But I
don't think you'll get out tomorrow or the day after."

"I don't think so, either."

She glanced at him. "You were nice to Mr. Hickman
this morning. He enjoyed talking to you." Why had she
brought up Mr. Hickman when the elderly man was
clearly trying to matchmake?

"Edwin Hickman is an interesting fellow, and I

enjoyed talking to him, too. He told me more about Lamont Nealey."

"Pay no attention to whatever Mr. Hickman said about Lamont."

"He said Lamont takes you out about once every three months. He also said you've told him you'll probably marry Lamont someday."

"Mr. Hickman exaggerates, and he doesn't remember accurately. Lamont and I go out when we want. Going out occasionally is good and makes it special," she said, thinking it really wasn't special, just a change from her routine to go to a show she wanted to see or Lamont wanted to attend. She had no intention of sounding as if she wanted Josh to ask her out, although she didn't think there was any chance of that ever happening. He should have no interest in her or a town like Beckett. Not the cosmopolitan Josh Calhoun, head of Calhoun Hotels.

"As for marrying Lamont, that may happen someday. We're compatible, we've known each other forever and Lamont is ideal. He's grown up here, works here and doesn't want to leave here. That description fits me also. How many men would feel that way?"

"Have you ever heard the old saying 'opposites attract'?" Josh asked with a faint smile.

"I've heard the saying, but it's no part of my life. Lamont is the ideal man for me—very plain tastes, will never leave Beckett, tied to his family—which in his case is only his mother and a married aunt and her family. We're alike, we've known each other since we were children and neither of us is in a rush to marry. That's all I want."

"You're damn easy to please. More than any woman I've ever known."

"I'm sure I'm not like women you've known," she

said, smiling at him. "I know you can't imagine such a simple life as Lamont's or mine, but that's what I know and like. My mother falls into your 'opposites attract' category. My dad was a charmer, a traveling salesman. He was delightful, but oh, so unreliable, and after three kids, he finally left Mom for another woman he met in California. When he did, it broke her heart, and I don't like to remember that time. It was sad for all of us."

"That doesn't mean all men with personalities like your dad's won't be faithful or honor their marriage vows."

"I'm not sure I believe that. I've heard he now has his fourth wife. I don't want someone like that in my life. What about you, Josh? You're single. I seriously doubt if you're searching for your opposite," she said, amused. "You would be bored beyond measure."

"I suppose you're right," he said, smiling with her. "Right now, I'm not at the point where I care to get tied down. You're already tied down with this inn— that's 24/7. You work more than I do, and that's saying something."

"It doesn't seem like work," she said. "I enjoy the people and the job and taking care of the inn. I enjoy my family and Mr. Hickman, Aunt Trudy and Aunt Millie."

"Well, you're good at what you do, and I will be forever grateful for getting to stay here."

"I'd better get moving because lunch will come before you know it." As she walked away, her back tingled, and she had to fight the urge to glance over her shoulder. She was certain he watched her. But what was he thinking?

Along with sandwiches that Josh helped her make for lunch, she had a pot of vegetable soup, a salad and choices of chocolate or lemon cake, yogurt or cookies for dessert.

All the time she worked, she couldn't lose the sharp awareness she had of him. She thought it would diminish as she got accustomed to him being at the inn and working with her, but it didn't diminish one tiny degree.

Far from it—as she felt a constant, tingling consciousness of him wherever he was or whatever he did.

Through lunch she tried to ignore her fluttering insides. Afterward they sat and talked for an hour over cups of coffee. Then Josh helped her get dinner started, peeling potatoes while she prepared a roast. By the time they cleaned up and sat down with cold drinks, the delicious smell of the roast and potatoes in a slow cooker filled the kitchen.

"You've been such a help. I'll owe you when you leave."

"No, you won't. Your inn has been a lifesaver."

A clock chimed in the hall. "Oh, my word. I need to check the inn's email account before dinner. They begin to drift down after five for a cocktail," she said, standing and carrying her glass to the sink.

Turning, she almost bumped into him as he did the same.

"Sorry," she said, causing him to smile.

"Slow down. I'll help with serving dinner and with the cocktails. Where do you keep glasses? Do you have a bar?"

"There's a small bar in the corner of the back room. We were in the living room last night because of the piano, but usually we gather in the back sitting room because it's the largest. Through that door. I'll hurry and be in the kitchen in about twenty minutes."

He set his glass in the sink and caught up with her

to head toward his room. They parted at the door, and she rushed on to her entrance. She had spent the day with him, and it had flown by swiftly. She liked being with him, still had the dizzying response to him physically and anticipated with a growing eagerness being with him again soon.

She knew that Josh would disappear from her life, but it had been fun while he was here—because she wasn't letting herself fall for him.

She showered and dressed in another thick sweater, this time pink. She pulled on jeans and her suede boots and brushed her hair into a fresh ponytail.

With an uncustomary eagerness, Abby went to the kitchen to check on dinner and set the table. Josh was already there in a charcoal sweater, chinos and his Western boots, his straight, short brown hair neatly combed. He hadn't shaved today, and a faint dark shadow of stubble on his jaw gave him a rugged look and added to his appeal. He was handsome enough that she had to fight the temptation to stare. Once again, Josh was helpful, setting the dining room table without even being asked.

When the first guests came downstairs, Josh left to serve them drinks. She was busy all through dinner and afterward until the kitchen was clean and everything put away. She heard Josh join the guests about five minutes before she did. As she went into the big sitting room, she could see through an open door some of the men playing pool in the billiards room. In the sitting room, some of the little girls sat at a table with crayons and coloring books. Other kids worked a puzzle, while two teens were busy with their phones. She looked at the fire Josh had built before dinner and saw it would soon go out.

Crossing the room to a game table, she stopped beside Josh, who sat playing cards with Mr. Hickman.

"Can I trade places briefly with you and get you to bring in some logs from the woodpile so the fire doesn't die?"

"Sure," Josh said, standing. "It's your turn, Mr. Hickman."

"I know, I know," he said without looking up.

She smiled at Josh, who stood only inches away. She hoped he never realized the extent of the reaction she had to his presence. "The woodpile is below the east windows of this room," she said, pointing. "You can go out through the kitchen. Thanks."

She slid onto his seat and watched Mr. Hickman. His wrinkled hands were poised on the edge of the board as he studied his cards.

They each played several cards before Josh returned carrying logs. He paused near Abby. "Folks, there is a huge full moon that you can see rising over the horizon if you step outside and look to the east," he announced, looking around the room. He glanced at Abby. "It's marvelous out," he added, setting down the logs. "Let's go look and then I'll build a fire."

"Mr. Hickman, do you want to look at the moon?" she asked.

"Of course," he said. "I'll get my coat. It's supposed to be seventeen degrees tonight."

"Can I go upstairs and get it for you, sir?" Josh asked.

"It's down here in the hall closet," Abby said.

"Thank you very much anyway," Mr. Hickman said to Josh.

Once Mr. Hickman had on his coat, Abby got hers out of the hall closet, and Josh held it for her as she slipped into it. "Ready, Mr. Hickman?"

"Ready," he replied.

Abby linked arms with Mr. Hickman and was aware

of Josh moving to the other side of him. Josh held the door, and finally they stepped out onto the porch and walked around the house. Her guests were clustered there, some huddled together because they hadn't bothered to get their coats. Some gasped at the wintry scene. The wind had finally died, and the snow had stopped falling. It was a cold, clear night, and an enormous moon hovered over the horizon. The moon was a huge white ball with gray patterns on its surface. Nobody had walked through the snow beyond the house yet, and it was pristine, glistening in the bright moonlight.

"Just a minute," Abby said, releasing Mr. Hickman's arm and walking to one side of the crowd. "Folks, we have an old Texas legend about the moon. If you'll move over here on the porch where I'm standing, you can see two oak trees in the yard with entwined branches." She waited a moment as the group clustered around her.

"The full moon shining on those oak trees sometimes casts a heart-shaped shadow. There's an old legend here that if two people kiss in that shadow, they will fall in love with each other for the rest of their lives. If you want to see the shadow, you have to stand on this part of the porch, or if you're in the yard, stand right in front of the porch at this place."

"Has anyone who has stayed at the inn ever seen it and kissed in the shadow?" someone asked.

"Oh, yes," Abby said. "Including my grandparents. My grandfather died very young, so my grandmother wasn't married long, but she always loved him and has never remarried." Talking softly, people turned to watch as shadows across the snow changed gradually.

"So, have you ever kissed in this shadow?" a deep voice asked beside Abby. She turned to glance at Josh, thankful for the darkness that hid a blush warming her cheeks.

"No, I haven't. There—look, Josh, I think the shadow is forming," she whispered, watching the shifting dark patterns on the dazzling white snow. The crowd became silent, seemingly transfixed.

There was a collective gasp when a heart-shaped shadow became visible. People began to call out about it and hold up their phones to take pictures. One couple ran down the porch steps to kiss in the shadow. Two more couples joined them, and little kids laughed and clapped. Someone whistled.

"We can't waste that," Josh said, taking her hand and hurrying down the steps.

"Josh—"

"It's only a kiss," he said, rushing to stand in the shadow of the heart and pull her to him.

"This is absurd," she said, laughing, her own heart pounding wildly. "Suppose it comes true? We don't even know each other. You're tempting fate. We might not like each other—"

"We'll find out," he said, wrapping his arms around her and leaning down to kiss her. His mouth covered hers.

Shocked, excited, caught off guard, she thought this kiss was the craziest thing she had ever done in her quiet, ordinary life. And then she stopped thinking and was consumed by his kiss, which built a fire deep within her. She couldn't get her breath. She became oblivious to the cold, the snow and the people around her, as well as the knowledge that she barely knew Josh. All she was aware of was his mouth on hers, his arms banding her tightly, holding her against his solid, warm length.

She had never been kissed like this, held like this. She wrapped her arms around his neck and kissed him passionately in return. The reason for their kiss vanished. All she knew was Josh, his hard strength, his tongue that took her breath completely and stirred her desire to a level she hadn't experienced before.

With Josh's kiss, her world and her life underwent a change as subtle as the shifting shadows around her, but in another way, a change far more monumental. Desire burned hotly, enveloping her, permeating her being. She clung tightly to him, kissing him in a way she had never kissed any other man.

At some point she realized where she was and what she was doing. With an effort she stepped back. As they broke apart, people clapped again, laughed and whistled. She was thankful for the darkness, because her face burned from embarrassment as she tried to smile but couldn't.

For once, Josh's ever-ready smile didn't appear. He stared at her.

"We drew a crowd," she said quietly. "That shadow is long gone."

"Yeah."

She turned away. Josh caught her hand as people clapped again. "Bow," he said. "We have an audience. Let's join the fun, and the moment will pass. Sort of."

She curtsied as Josh bowed again.

The crowd broke up. Kids were tossing snowballs, and several had started a snowman. The snow crunched beneath their feet as they walked back to the inn. They stopped to accompany Mr. Hickman.

"Josh is an enterprising young man," Mr. Hickman said, laughter in his voice. "I shall try to prevail upon him to go fishing with me."

"That would be nice," she said, thinking Josh would never come back to Beckett, and he probably was too busy to fish often. When he did, she suspected he flew to Colorado or Idaho or some location where fishing was much more challenging and satisfying than a stocked pond in a small west Texas town.

They went inside and put away their coats. "Want to finish our game?" Josh asked Mr. Hickman.

"Yes, indeed, and then it will be my bedtime."

"See you later," Josh said to her, and the two men turned to go to their game. One of the guests stopped to ask her if they would be having cocoa later.

"Yes. Would you and your family like some now? I can make it now just as easily."

"That would be wonderful. I'll come help."

"You don't need to. I'll announce it as soon as it's ready. It doesn't really take long."

"Thank you, Abby. We all look forward to your homemade hot cocoa," the petite blonde said. "I'll tell my family and the others."

Abby hurried to the kitchen, trying to focus on making hot cocoa for everyone and keeping Josh's kiss out of her thoughts for now. She failed to stop thinking about him, but she had made cocoa so many times in her life, she could do what she needed to without much thought.

Finally she escaped to her room for a moment to catch her breath. As soon as she shut her door, she leaned against it. Remembering Josh's kiss, she closed her eyes. Why did she have this huge reaction to Josh, of all people, who would go out of her life as swiftly as he had come into it?

Three

Abby crossed the room to look into the mirror. She should look different, but she didn't. She felt different, as if Josh's kiss had somehow in some subtle manner changed her permanently.

She knew she had lived a sheltered, quiet life, but she had no idea a man's kiss could ignite a raging fire in her.

It was just as well he would soon leave. Occasionally men would stay at the inn who were charming and single. They would flirt and ask her out, and she had always turned them down. There had never been anybody she had particularly wanted to go out with, and she had never had a reason to cause any ripples in her relationship with Lamont. She had always felt secure, comfortable and reasonably happy with him, but was she cutting deep joy and fun out of her life? There were other nice guys in Beckett and areas close around. Answering Josh's questions about Lamont made her realize her romantic relationship with her old friend was almost nonexistent. Had she let the hurt caused by her father influence her too strongly? She went out with Lamont because it was convenient and easy.

Josh had not asked her out, and she didn't expect he would. Any day now he'd pack and go, and she would never see him again. How long would it take to forget his kiss?

Was that going to dim her relationship with Lamont, whose kisses were bland and far from exciting? Was she missing out on life, as Josh had accused her?

Was she settling for a dull, uneventful future with Lamont simply because it was safe and convenient? And was it even fair to Lamont?

Should she and Lamont date other people? If Josh asked her out, would she feel free to accept if she and Lamont didn't have an agreement to see others?

For the first time, she wanted out of the arrangement she had simply drifted into with Lamont. With uncustomary impulsiveness, she called him on his cell.

"Have you got a moment to talk, Lamont?"

"I need a short break, so yes, I'll take a minute. Why do taxes seem to have more rules each year?"

"I don't know much about that. Lamont, I've been thinking about us, that we should start going out with other people. We've sort of wandered into a relationship that I'm having some second thoughts about."

"Abby, we're just alike, so we're very compatible. And this is a terrible time for me to make major changes in my life. Maybe you should rethink this. I'm sorry if I've neglected you somewhat, but we don't usually go out during tax season, at least not in late March."

"I want to be free to date others, and I think it would do you good to do so, too. We may be in a rut." There was a long period of silence. She hated to upset him, but she still felt she should break it off with him, at least for a while.

"If that's what you want," he said. "Let's go to dinner and discuss it, but it will have to be in a few weeks."

"We can discuss it more when you're finished with taxes, but I want to agree to see others."

"Fine," he said and gave an audible sigh. "I better get back. We'll talk about this again."

"Sure, Lamont," she said, feeling better. She put away her phone, realizing she had just made what might be a life-changing decision. A decision based on a kiss from a man who was almost a stranger. Even so, she didn't regret it.

Taking a deep breath, she turned to go back and join the guests to see if anyone needed anything. Josh and Mr. Hickman had just finished their game as Abby joined them.

"We've each won a game now," Mr. Hickman said.

"Actually, you've won two and I've won one."

"We'll play again sometime, I hope." Mr. Hickman stood. "I think I should turn in. I'll see both of you at breakfast. I enjoyed the games, Josh. Thanks."

"You're welcome," Josh said. "I enjoyed them, too. We'll see you in the morning."

"Good night," Abby said. As soon as Mr. Hickman was gone, she turned to Josh. "There's hot cocoa and hot cider in the kitchen."

"At this point in my life, I'd like a cold beer."

"I think we can fill that order," she said as they walked to the kitchen. "Look in the fridge. If we're out, there's another fridge in the pantry."

"I'll find it." He got a beer, uncapped it and sipped, then set it on the counter. He picked up dishes people had left at the table, carrying them to the sink. "I'll check the dining room for dishes that need to be washed."

Five minutes later, dishwasher running, he pulled out a chair. "Sit here and we can talk where it's quiet. No cards, no piano, no movie."

She hesitated a moment. The more time she spent with him, the more she liked him. She should thank him and go because the man was a threat to her peaceful life, even though he didn't know it or intend to be. She stared at him as she debated with herself. Had Josh caused her to want to go out with others, to change her basic lifestyle? How much upheaval was he causing in her life?

"This isn't a monumental decision," he said, looking more intently at her. "Or is it? And if it's monumental—why? What are you concerned about?"

"Of course not," she said, her cheeks flushing. "I don't think anyone in there will miss me, so I'll stay. I'm ready for a little quiet." She sat quickly, sipping a cup of steaming cocoa, aware of his curious gaze on her.

"You've been good to play cards with Mr. Hickman," she said.

"He's a nice man. I haven't played cards since I was a little kid."

She smiled, relieved to be on an impersonal topic.

"By the way, Edwin asked me to come back and go fishing with him in about a week or later, depending on the weather. It's spring, and the weather should warm up. The snow will disappear soon."

"So, are you coming back?"

"Not to fish," he said. Even though she felt a twinge of disappointment over his answer, she was not surprised and knew it was for the best.

"Later this spring, I'll return to Beckett, but only to

pick up Edwin. I asked him to go fishing in Colorado for a weekend—we can stay in my cabin there. I'll fly us up. His health is good enough for him to go, isn't it?"

Startled that he would take Mr. Hickman to Colorado, she barely thought about her answer. "Yes, as far as I know. He seems fine, just elderly."

"He's enthused and sounds knowledgeable about fly-fishing, so we should have a good time. I'll ask him to check with his doc about the altitude change in case he needs to spend a night somewhere on the way."

"He goes to the doctor for regular checkups, so I'm pretty certain he wouldn't accept if he didn't think he was healthy enough to make the trip. He does like to fish. That's very nice of you," she said, staring at him. She would never have guessed that Josh would have asked Mr. Hickman to fly to Colorado to go fishing. "Frankly, I'm surprised. You don't seem the type to hang out with Mr. Hickman."

Josh smiled at her. "I'm a man of many facets—stick around and you'll see."

"I don't doubt you for a minute," she said. "Even so, that amazes me. I'm very impressed," she added, realizing Josh was not only appealing, helpful, fun, sexy—but also a very nice person. Once again, she thought that she should stop spending so much time with him because she could quickly and easily fall in love with him—a love that definitely would not be reciprocated.

"Well, now, that is satisfying. Interestingly, I've done some business with one of Edwin's sons in Dallas and see all three of his sons at parties. They have a successful business that Edwin started."

"I know he has five grandkids and he misses all of them."

"He likes it here because he has old friends here, but

he's beginning to think about moving to Dallas. To my way of thinking, he would be better off near his family, but that's Mr. Hickman's business. My folks are in California, so I'm in about the same situation, only younger. My parents are younger than Mr. Hickman, and they're very busy."

"He should have a wonderful time going fishing."

They sat in silence while Josh sipped his beer.

"Were your stories true tonight about the people you've known who have kissed in that shadow?"

"Yes, they were true," she said, surprised he would ask such a question. "Why would I make them up?"

"It's good for business. Sort of a special touch for this inn."

She laughed. "Goodness, no, I wouldn't make them up for business. I never know if that shadow will appear. We can go years when it doesn't. A lot of things have to be just right and shadows change as the earth turns, so it's very fleeting when it happens."

"Have people ever kissed in that shadow when they met each other barely twenty-four hours before?"

"No one whom I've known about."

"Has anyone you know about ever kissed in the shadow, married and then separated?"

"No. All of them stayed married, so see, you tempted fate. But take heart. We don't know each other, so I doubt if we would count. I expect our kiss to be meaningless."

"My kiss, meaningless—that's the first time I've been told that. I'm slipping. I used to get a better reaction," he said, his brown eyes twinkling. She had to fight the temptation to look at his mouth.

"You know you did get a better reaction," she flung

back at him, even though she had intended to stop flirting with him.

"Did I really now?" he asked.

"Don't act surprised," she said, then decided to change the subject to one that would keep her from kissing him again. "Tomorrow or the next day, the roads will be plowed and you can go on your way. And my brother and sister will be here to help."

There was a knock at the open door, and a guest stepped into the room. "I'm sorry to disturb you."

"We were just talking. Can I help you with something?" Abby asked.

"Do you have the old movie *The African Queen*?" the short blonde asked.

"Yes, we do. You can't find it?"

As she shook her head, Abby stood. "I'll come look. I'll be right back, Josh." She left the kitchen, leaving Josh sipping his beer, his eyes still twinkling.

Josh thought about their kiss. Her kiss had almost knocked him off his feet, and he hoped her reaction to him had been as intense. He'd thought she wasn't his type, but kissing her had changed his view of her. Her kisses melted him. There was no way he was flying out of Beckett without the certainty of coming back to be with her, to kiss her and to make love with her. As far as he was concerned, seduction was on his schedule.

He liked being with her. Maybe it was the laid-back atmosphere—no business, no calls, a different world for him—but he wanted to be with her. She had a big job running the inn and keeping people happy in this storm when they were stranded, and she did it with ease.

She returned to the kitchen, and he watched her ponytail swing as she walked across the room. She had a jaunty walk as if life were delightful and she intended to enjoy it. His gaze rested on her mouth while he thought about their kiss again.

"Did you find the movie?"

"Oh, yes. Someone had slipped it under the sofa." She smiled. "Pretty easy task."

"Do you ever take time off?" he asked, still studying her. What would she look like with her hair down and makeup on?

"I get someone in the family to cover for me if I need to take time off, but there are quiet days and times we only have two or three guests and some days when there are none, so it evens out. This is my life—always has been. I started helping my grandmother when I was about ten, maybe younger," she said.

"You don't ever want to go somewhere new? New York? Paris? London?" he asked, thinking there was nothing they had in common. "Is there something you'd like to do that you've never done?" He was certain he had never really known anyone with so few demands or wishes about life. He didn't date women who led the type of life Abby did. She was a homebody and shouldn't hold an instant's worth of attention from him, but all he had to do was think about kissing her and he got hot, shaken and lost in memories of their only kiss.

"I can't think of anything that I long to do."

He looked at her as if he had suddenly discovered someone from another world. "Surely there's something."

She smiled at him. "Sometimes I used to wonder what it would be like to go to Vienna to a castle or a palace. When I was little, I would imagine that I was in a palace at a ball. The music was always a waltz. I wore one of those beautiful dresses. I probably saw a movie with that scene, and I love music and particularly a waltz. Somehow at local dances, they never seem to play a waltz. Lots of two-steps, lots of square dances, no waltzes," she said, looking beyond him as if she had forgotten his presence.

He thought of the castles he had seen, the waltzes he had danced, thinking how waltzes were old-fashioned and not his favorite dance.

She smiled at him, focusing on him again. "No, I don't plan to go to foreign places. I see movies and it looks fun, but I don't really yearn to travel."

"You lead a simple life, and you're damn easy to please."

"Like I've said, my life is tied up in family and people here." She glanced around. "Want something to drink?"

"I still have my beer. What would you like?"

"One more cup of hot cocoa if I have any left. If not, just a glass of milk with a little honey in it."

"I can start another fire in my room—which is really your room," he said, wanting to be alone with her. "Why don't we sit there to talk? No one should need you the rest of this evening."

"Sure," she said as she poured her hot chocolate.

They finally settled on the floor in the living area of her suite with a blazing fire in the fireplace, cold beer, hot cocoa and a bowl of popcorn. Josh had pulled a coffee table near the hearth as a table for the drinks and popcorn.

They sat in silence a few moments. She watched the fire, her profile to him. His gaze traveled over her smooth skin, long, light-brown eyelashes, a straight nose and full, heart-shaped lips. He paused, looking at her lips while desire built and he fought an inner battle.

She wasn't his type of woman and he wasn't her type of man—in all ways except one. One that he couldn't resist as he thought about their kiss.

He could not stop wanting to kiss her again. Kiss her and more, so much more. She was sexy, responsive, plus a bundle of nice and capable traits. So many that she was beginning to seem like a very special woman with a lot more substance than some women he'd spent a great deal of time with.

"Tell me more about your family," she said, breaking into his thoughts. "Do they all live near you in Dallas? Do they work with you?"

"My brother Mike is a rancher. He just married a woman who is a neonatal nurse, although she's not working now. She's expecting, and Mike has a little boy, Scotty. Mike's first wife died of cancer."

"I'm so sorry to hear that. It's nice that he's remarried."

"He seems very happy, and so does Scotty. I think the marriage has been great for my brother and my nephew. It was good for Savannah, too, because she had a broken engagement and that ex-fiancé is the father of her child, although Mike will adopt the baby."

"That's a blessing for all concerned."

"My brother Jake is in the energy business and married to Madison Milan, an artist."

"I've met her. She stayed here once, and she's very nice. She wouldn't remember me."

"She is nice, and they're happy. It's a good marriage because for generations our two families have had a nasty feud, beginning with the cattlemen after the Civil War. The feud is fading, especially with Jake and Madison's marriage. And a distant relative of ours, Destiny, married a Milan—Wyatt Milan, the sheriff of Verity."

"Sounds as if the feud is over."

"Unfortunately, it's not. My sister, Lindsay, is neighbors with a Milan, and those two fight like two bears with one piece of meat. Since Wyatt became sheriff, he's been able to tone it down a little, but not much, so the old feud is alive and well."

"You have quite a history, and your Texas ancestors go back as far as ours do," she said, smiling at him. "Do you stay at your ranch often?"

"I don't. I'd like to, but I'm too busy. That's the life I really love, and I'll move to the ranch to live someday."

"The future has a way of becoming the past very quickly. Perhaps you should take more time for your ranch if you really like that life."

"Right now that day seems mighty far in the future."

"My family is close—as you can guess since Mom lives next door and my grandmother lives here at the inn, although she stays at Mom's house a lot of the time. That's where she has been a lot this winter, and right now she's gone to visit another relative."

"Is your mom okay in this storm? Does she need anything?"

"No. I checked, and she has groceries. Right now with everyone snowed in, she doesn't need the drive shoveled. I talk to her every day on the phone. This snow keeps her out of work, which is probably a much-needed rest for her. She has a hair salon and is usually busy."

"What about your siblings?"

"My brother and sister are both on spring break—and it's a good time to be gone. The snow is keeping them from getting back home."

Of all the women he had known, why was it a nurturer like Abby who set him on fire with her kisses?

The most unlikely female he had crossed paths with attracted him—and she must be attracted to some degree to him. He couldn't imagine why she would give him five seconds of attention, because she had already told him she avoided men who traveled or reminded her of the type of life her father had—but she *did* give him attention.

It was after one in the morning when she stood and picked up the tray of dishes. "It's late. I'll turn in now."

"I'll carry the tray," he said, taking it from her.

"I need to lock up and turn off lights. People leave them on." They walked down the hall to the kitchen.

"If the forecasts are correct," she said, "we should have better weather by Tuesday. Maybe they'll open the roads and you'll get to go home."

"Don't sound so hopeful," he said, teasing her, and she smiled at him.

"Believe me, I've always been aware that when the snow goes, you will, too. That's the way of all my guests, no matter how good a time they've had here."

"I'm guessing a lot of your guests have been here before or will come back again."

"You're right, fortunately. People like staying here. They do come back, and a lot of them keep in touch with us. We get Christmas cards from all over the United States, which makes me happy."

"I'll send you a card."

"By next Christmas, you may not remember me, much less remember to send a card," she said, sounding amused.

He turned to face her, blocking her way. "I'll remember you," he said in a husky voice, knowing that he would. He wondered how long it would take for him to forget her or if he ever really would, a thought that surprised him.

Her faint smile faded as her eyes widened. Heat streaked like lightning across his loins. He stood holding the tray of dishes with his hands full. He set the tray on the counter and turned to take her into his arms. "This is why I won't forget you for a long, long time," he said and kissed her, pulling her tightly against him as he leaned over her.

As before when he had kissed her, she held him just as tightly, pressing against him, kissing him in return, another hot kiss that blasted him with desire. He wanted her in his bed. Kisses to die for—the description flitted through his mind.

"Josh," she whispered, stepping out of his embrace. She was as breathless as he was, and her lips were red from his kiss. He wanted to wrap his arms around her again, but knew he shouldn't. She needed to lock up and turn off lights, and she would stick to that agenda. He placed the dishes in the dishwasher while she went to the sitting room to switch off lights. When she returned, she checked the back door.

"I think everything is off and locked, so with no more chores, let's go to bed," she said, switching off the kitchen light, leaving only the hall light.

"Oh, darlin', I am definitely ready," he drawled.

Glancing over her shoulder at him, she laughed. "Cool it—poor choice of words on my part. I'm going to bed—alone. You do as you please and cool your overactive—" she paused "—imagination."

He grinned as he strolled down the hall beside her. "You can't blame me. Hope springs eternal and all that."

"I might as well start planning tomorrow's activities, because I'm guessing it'll be a busy day."

"You're changing the subject."

"As fast as I can," she said as they walked into his room. She kept going to the adjoining door to the rest of her suite. She turned to face him. "It's been a fun and interesting day."

As he walked over to her, she opened the connecting door to her room. He caught her arm, turning her. "It's been an unforgettable day and night. We kissed in a shadow that is supposed to change our lives. Now we wait and see."

"It's a legend. That doesn't mean it comes true. I think it probably makes a difference if you're already in love when you kiss," she said. Her voice had softened and had a breathless quality now, a reaction to their conversation or to his touch or to his standing so close—he didn't know. All he knew was that she always had a response to him.

"We can't end this day without another kiss," he whispered. Before she could answer him or try to walk away, he placed his mouth on hers.

He stood kissing her until she finally moved out of his arms.

"I don't know why we have this effect on each other," she whispered.

"We do, and I find it fascinating and irresistible."

"Watch out. It may be as risky to your way of life as it is to mine. You tempted fate tonight, and you're still doing it."

"How am I still doing it when I'm just standing here?" he asked in a husky voice.

"Good night, Josh," she said a little more forcefully and stepped into her room, closing the door.

"Good night, Abby," he said, certain she stood close

enough on the other side of the door to hear him. "You didn't answer my question," he added.

He was hot, aroused, aching with desire. He wanted her, and he wanted to hold her and make love for hours. He did not want to tell her goodbye yet.

Later, as he lay on the sofa, he stared into the dark and tried to avoid thinking about her in bed only mere yards away with a door between them. In addition to the hot chemistry, she had jolted his busy lifestyle, moving him into a slower pace, making him think more about his life as a rancher. It had always seemed something in the far distant future when he was older, but was he missing out on life, as she had said? He definitely thought she was missing out on life in many ways, yet in others, she might have a happier lifestyle than he did. That thought shocked him.

He rose slightly to see if there was a light beneath her door. It was dark, so she was in bed. That thought was not conducive to his sleep.

What would happen if he knocked on the door? Some women would tell him to come in, but he was certain Abby would tell him to go away and she would see him in the morning.

He sat up and wondered if sleep would come. The firewood was ashes with a few glowing orange embers, and he watched them sparkle while he remembered holding her until he groaned and ran his hand through his hair. He looked at the door between them again. Was she on the other side sleeping peacefully without a thought about him?

As she pulled on flannel pajamas and then laid out her blue sweater, a fresh pair of jeans and thick knee socks with her suede boots for tomorrow, Abby could only think of Josh. She ached with wanting him. She wanted his arms around her, his kisses, his lovemaking. But that was hopeless and the way to big heartbreak.

She wanted to go on with her routine life when he left, as happy as she was before she met him. She had the feeling life as usual wasn't going to happen again. Josh had come into her world and changed everything.

She had known Lamont's kisses were not exciting, but she had thought perhaps no man's kisses would ever seem exciting to her. She enjoyed Lamont, but on a whole different level and to a lesser degree than she did Josh. Lamont had never sent her pulse galloping or kissed her until she shook with desire. She never sat talking and laughing for hours with Lamont. They were comfortable, but sometimes they sat together for an hour or more without saying ten words to each other.

She would never feel the same about any other man now that she had known Josh. His fiery kiss had changed her world, making her reconsider her relationship with Lamont. She was glad she had talked to Lamont. They could be cheating themselves by limiting themselves to such a dry, emotionally lacking relationship. After Josh's kiss, she didn't want to keep the status quo with Lamont.

She sighed as she contemplated how Josh had so swiftly changed her views of life. It was a good thing Josh would soon leave. Otherwise, she would fall in love—deeply in love—for the first time in her life. Josh was excitement, passion, dreams. How long would it take her to forget him?

Sunday morning Abby stirred to sunshine showing around the edges of the shutters that covered her windows. Stretching, she climbed out of bed to open the

shutters and look out a partially frosted window at spar-
kling white snow. The sun was brilliant, dazzling on
the glistening white. She smiled and hurried to shower
and dress and start the day.

By the time she got to the kitchen, Josh already had
the table set in the dining room, and he was outside,
shoveling snow along the drive and walk. She stared at
him a moment, shaking her head, thinking that Lamont
would not be shoveling snow or setting a table. Her cell
buzzed, and she saw it was Lamont, which surprised
her. She read his text message and saw that he would
come by to see Mr. Hickman tomorrow morning.

Soon enough, Mr. Hickman arrived, greeting Abby
as he came through the buffet line in the kitchen.

"Good morning. It's a beautiful day even though everyone will still be snowed in."

"You're chipper this morning," she said, smiling at
him.

"I'm thinking about the fishing trip Josh has prom-
ised. That's an exciting event in my life. I love to
fish, and the thought of dropping a line in a Colorado
stream—I can't tell you how marvelous that is. He's a
remarkable young man to take me fishing. By the way,
where is he this morning?"

"He's shoveling snow off the front drive. I'd tell him
to stop since he's a guest, but he'll just go ahead, so I
didn't even bother. If he'd waited, I could have called
to get some boys to shovel it later."

"According to the news, everything in town is still
closed, including the roads, so there's not a rush. The
highway is shut down because of high drifts. It won't
open until they can get it cleaned off."

"I suspect it's useless to tell Josh to stop."

"Ah, he's a good person. I would go help him, but I've reached a point in life where I can't."

"He wouldn't let you help. I wouldn't want you even to try, so don't think about it. He's doing what he wants to do, and neither you nor I can talk him out of it."

"I'm not about to talk him out of it. I just regret I can't join him."

"You're nice, too. Enjoy your breakfast. I'll bring coffee."

She was serving the coffee when she heard Josh come in the back door. Eagerness to see him made her smile. He had done one more thing to win her heart.

Four

"Thank you, but you shouldn't have cleared the drive. I could have found some kids to shovel it. Tomorrow Lamont is coming over if he can, but he would never think of shoveling the drive."

"He doesn't shovel for himself or his mother?" Josh asked as he pulled off snow-covered boots and removed his thick jacket. He had on his heavy knit brown sweater and jeans. Once again, he hadn't shaved, and it still took Abby's breath away to look at him.

"He pays a neighbor kid to shovel their walk and drive," she said. "Tommy is eleven years old and it takes him a while, but he gets it done and doesn't charge much."

"So Lamont is a tight accountant?" Josh asked.

"I guess you'd say so, yes. He's also Mr. Hickman's and my aunts' accountant, and that's why he's coming here."

Josh paused in hanging his gloves on a hat tree. "He's not coming to see you?"

"No," she answered, smiling. "We've grown up seeing each other. He's got some papers about taxes for Mr. Hickman. This is Lamont's busiest time of year." She headed toward the kitchen. "Come get breakfast. Everyone else has eaten or is finishing. You can sit in the kitchen with me if you want while I finish cleaning. Thanks again, Josh, for doing the drive. It's big, and that's a major job for anybody."

"I work out, and I don't mind. You'll need it clear tomorrow if people start leaving."

"You're right there," she said, walking into the kitchen with him. "Help yourself. I'll be back in a minute," she said as she went to the dining room. Everyone had finished eating, so she cleared the table and returned to the kitchen as Josh sat.

She rinsed dishes to place them in the dishwasher, washed and dried her hands and poured herself a cup of steaming coffee, which she carried to the table to sit across from Josh while he ate breakfast.

"Josh, Mr. Hickman is so happy about the fishing trip. He even sounds younger and peppier this morning."

"I'm glad. I'm looking forward to getting away for it myself."

"Oh, I meant to ask, did you buy the horse you came to Beckett to get?"

"Yes, I did, from Jim Lee Hearne."

"I know Jim. He recently married."

"Right. He and his wife are selling their horses and moving to California. He has one really promising cutting horse, and I bought it from him."

A woman appeared in the doorway. "Abby, I'm sorry

to interrupt you, but do you have a small bandage? Micah cut his finger on his broken toy."

"Sure," Abby replied, standing. "Excuse me, Josh," she said, leaving to help her guest.

When she returned, Josh had gone and had put her empty cup and saucer into the dishwasher. Of course, he had.

During the morning, Abby did chores, talked at length with her mother on the phone and then spent her time getting lunch ready. As soon as she started, Josh appeared. She was happy for his help and acutely aware of him.

In the afternoon, people played games while Josh helped her get dinner ready. He played checkers with Mr. Hickman and spent some time talking to various guests. She realized Josh had made a point to meet and talk to everyone staying at the inn, including the kids. One more facet so different from Lamont, who would have kept to himself.

Again, Abby was aware of him as he helped her with dinner. The more she knew him, the more the awareness grew, instead of diminishing as she kept expecting.

Finally, after all the chores were done, the food eaten and the kitchen cleaned, he turned to her. "Let's sit in your suite like we did last night. I've been with your guests and Edwin all day. I'm ready for some time with you where we're not working."

She smiled at him. "Sure. You've been great help."

"Let's go to your room and you can show me your appreciation," he said, leering at her in exaggeration and making her laugh.

"I'll give you a very nice pat on the back."

"A pat on the back isn't what I have in mind," he said,

getting a beer from the refrigerator. "We'll build a fire and have peace and quiet, just the two of us."

They sat talking in front of the fire with only one small lamp turned on. Josh was certain he would be able to leave tomorrow, and he kept thinking about telling her goodbye—something he didn't want to do.

Was his perspective warped because of his isolation, the storm, the full moon, the pressure he had been under for the past two weeks, the relaxation of being stranded in Beckett? Or was it her kisses that he couldn't stop thinking about?

His gaze ran over Abby, the blue sweater clinging to tempting curves, her low V-neck even more tempting. He'd like to take down her ponytail, but he didn't think she'd let him.

Goodbye seemed way too final.

"I hear the weather should clear tomorrow, so you may be able to go home."

"Now I have mixed feelings about that. This has been an unexpected holiday."

"Ah, that's good to hear. It's wonderful to sit back and enjoy life."

"I agree. It's also good to get out and really live," he said, touching her hand lightly with his fingers, even the slight contact electrifying.

When her lashes fluttered and her cheeks grew more pink, his pulse jumped a notch because of her instant response to his casual touch.

"Go to dinner with me Friday night," he said. The words were out as if the voice had come from somewhere besides himself, but once they were said, he wanted her to accept his invitation. He wanted her in his arms, and he wanted to kiss her again. He was traveling down a road he might regret, but he had no regrets about asking her out. She turned to stare at him with wide eyes and a slight frown. If he hadn't wanted her to accept so badly, he would have laughed over her expression—a disbelieving reaction he could not recall receiving in his adult life.

"You're coming back to Beckett?"

"Only to pick you up and take you someplace. You've worked hard these past days—why not enjoy a change? You get to relax for once."

"That's nice of you to ask. Where did you want to go?"

"You've rarely been out of Beckett," he said. "We can go to Dallas. We can go most anywhere you want to." They were silent a moment while he thought about where to take her that would be different for her.

"I have a new hotel opening this weekend in New York. I'll pick you up and we can fly to New York for the weekend. I can show you a tiny view of the city on Friday night, Saturday and early Sunday."

She laughed. "Me go to New York with you for the weekend? I think not, but thank you very much anyway."

"Wait a minute. Don't be so quick to say no," he said, deciding he had hit on something that would open up a whole new world for her. And give him a lot more time with her. "Think about it—I'll fly you to New York. I'm going anyway," he said. "You'll get to see things you've never seen before, and it'll be fun for both of us. No strings—just fun and getting to know each other better. You'll have your own suite, I promise. You'll be farther from me than you are tonight."

"Thank you, but I can't even imagine going off for the weekend with you or going to New York. You'll go home tomorrow and get back to your life, and you won't want to return to Beckett to take me to New York."

"Don't be so quick to turn me down," he said quietly, although a part of him thought she might be exactly right. "Get out and do something different for once and see if you like it. This might be the only time in your life you'll be in New York, the only time in your life you'll get out of your routine. I'll get you back home whenever you want. You can trust me."

She shook her head. "Our lives are too entirely different. I'm not the woman you want to take to New York for the weekend."

"You let me decide that one," he said. "The question is, do you want to go with me?"

The pink in her cheeks deepened, and he wondered if she blushed that easily all the time or if her blushes were only in reaction to him. "Give Lamont something to think about," Josh said, smiling at her. "C'mon, Abby, take a chance and live a little."

A faint smile flicked across her face. Impulsively, Josh reached over to take her cup of cocoa out of her hands. Her eyes widened as he set the cup on the table and turned back to pick her up and set her in his lap.

She opened her mouth, probably to protest. He kissed her before she could say anything. Wrapping his arms around her, he pulled her tightly against him. His heart pounded the minute his mouth covered hers. How could she turn him inside out like this? The question flitted through his thoughts and was gone. He wanted her. She responded instantly to him. She wound her arms around him and held him while she kissed him in return, a hot kiss that fanned the flames that had already been blazing.

As their kisses lengthened, desire thrummed, building to a heart-pounding need. He slid his hand beneath her thick sweater and up her smooth back, then around to her breast, caressing her so lightly through her bra. He cupped her full, warm breast, her softness making him hard. He was afraid to move too quickly because he didn't want her to stop him. He stroked her, shaking slightly with wanting her.

Her moan, her hip shifting against him, her softness and her wet, scalding kiss drove him to the edge. It took control to keep from peeling away her sweater or slipping his hand into her jeans—all moves that he suspected would end what she allowed right now.

Seduction, slow and sensual to build her need, was what he intended. As he kissed her he leaned away, slowly, caressing her with feathery strokes, her full breast a fiery temptation. She was warm, her skin smooth as velvet.

She tore her mouth from his. "Josh, you're going way too fast for me. I'm not ready for this. I can't—"

He raised his head to look at her. Her blue eyes were half-lidded, sultry, ready for sex. Again, she had a slight frown as if struggling with her own inner battle. He wanted to draw her back into his arms, hold her tightly and end her protests, which he suspected he might easily do.

He also wanted to please her, and he wanted her trust. He wanted her aching to make love as much as he did, so he sat quietly. He couldn't understand himself and his reaction to her. She shouldn't interest him in any way, for any reason. Her hair was in a perpetual ponytail and she wore no makeup. She had hardly been out of Beckett, never out of Texas. If she agreed to go to New York, she might not want more than a few kisses—hardly the sensual weekend he was hoping for.

He couldn't understand his own actions—something totally uncharacteristic for him. Why was he so attracted to her? Was it only the passionate kisses?

And yet he couldn't think of any other woman he had known whose kisses had had the effect on him that hers had. Plus, he liked to be with her.

She turned to face him. "My hot cocoa should be rather cold now, and your beer is probably warm. I'll go get some more."

He nodded and let her go, wanting to get some space between them, hoping to cool the strong urge to reach for her again.

He got up finally to go help her and met her as she was coming through the door. She carried a tray with cocoa, beer and popcorn and he took it from her, setting it on the coffee table and pulling it close as they sat on the floor in front of the fire again.

For a few minutes they made small talk. Then he lowered his beer. "You didn't give me an answer about the weekend. Go with me to New York." He leaned closer to her and caught her chin lightly in his hand. "Live a little, Abby. Life is a blast, so don't let it pass you by."

"Josh, it's crazy for me to think about going to New York with you."

"Why not with me? We have a good time together. It's just a weekend. No strings, Abby." He gazed into wide blue eyes filled with uncertainty.

"I promise you I will not sleep with you," she said in an earnest tone. "Knowing that, do you still want to take me to New York?"

He held back laughter that was as much at himself as her reaction. How did he get entangled with her? Worse, he was getting himself more involved by the minute. He had a chance right now to back off.

"I said no strings. We'll go and have fun."

She narrowed her eyes and leaned forward to stare intently at him. "Why do I suspect you of ulterior purposes?" she asked.

Amused, he leaned closer to her so their faces were only inches apart. "Because you like to kiss me, and you know I like to kiss you. I think you have to suspect yourself of ulterior purposes as well," he said softly, his gaze drifting down to her mouth.

"I guess I walked into that one," she said in a breathless voice. She sat back and gazed at him, looking as if she were thinking it over, so he remained quiet for a short time.

"Are you going with me?" he asked finally.

"Yes, I will," she said in a tone that sounded as if she had just agreed to rob a bank with him. "Friday night?"

"If you want to get in a little extra sightseeing, ask someone to cover for you and let's go Thursday. I'll bring you back when you want."

"Let's go Friday. That's long enough, and I can't believe I'm doing this."

He felt the same way, but he wouldn't tell her, ever. He smiled at her. "If you change your mind, that's fine, too. I'm adaptable." He sat back. "What would you like to eat on our first night there? Steak? Fish? Something foreign, exotic?"

She thought a moment. "Something French. French dishes always sound so delicious, and you know there's nowhere to eat any in Beckett. Cooking something from a recipe in a magazine doesn't always work out like I think it will. Something French would be fun, since you asked, but I can go anywhere you want."

"My house instead of New York?"

She laughed. "Now, that I hadn't thought about. I don't believe your house is on this trip's agenda. That one I'm not doing. It would be too intimate."

"I'm eating at your house this week."

"You and thirty-plus other people—that's a bit different. Only this weekend with you in New York. That's the same as if you'd told me you're taking me to the moon. It's just as unreal to me. I will be the talk of Beckett."

"They know you, and they know you'll still be you whether in New York or here."

"That's nice, Josh. I'm as dazzled as Edwin over the fishing trip. I'm going, but I can't believe it will happen."

He couldn't, either. "You've agreed. You've seen New York City in movies and on television—are there places you would particularly like to visit?"

"Maybe I should let you surprise me with your favorite places."

"I don't think so. I've been going since I was a little kid. You tell me what you want to see," he said, finding his thoughts drifting to where he could take her for dinner each night—someplace where they could dance. He was happy she said she would go. He would have her with him all weekend, and with her hot, sensual responses, he planned on seduction. By Saturday, she might even be eager.

It was two in the morning when Josh kissed her good-night and she went to her room. Finally she was alone and could think about the trip that she had accepted. As she changed into pajamas and took down her ponytail, she knew she couldn't cancel. She wanted to go. All too soon he would be out of her life forever, and she would be left with only memories of him and few of those. She intended to go to New York on Friday and have the time of her life, to store up memories for later.

She was too inexperienced to know much about men and love, but she suspected that she was already in love with Josh. When Josh kissed her beneath the rising moon, how could she resist him? And his appeal doubled when she found out he had asked Mr. Hickman to go fishing with him—something so many men Josh's age would never have taken time to do with someone elderly who was not a relative. All the help he had given her, the hours she had spent just sitting and talking to him—she liked him. He was handsome, sexy, exciting and a world of other good things. When he left, she would go back into the ordinary routine she had always had and would have for the rest of her life.

One weekend in New York—that was a thrill all by itself. One weekend in New York with Josh—that was beyond her wildest dreams. She thought of their kisses tonight and closed her eyes, tingling and wanting to be in his arms as she remembered his hand beneath her sweater, his caresses that she really hadn't wanted him to stop.

Even though she had broken off with Lamont, he was still in Beckett, still an old friend. Would this ruin a future relationship with Lamont? Did she really care if it would?

She would think about Lamont later. Right now the only man she wanted to think about was Josh.

Five

When she opened her eyes the next morning, she faced the realization that this was the day she would tell Josh goodbye—at least until Friday.

She went down early to get breakfast started, and Josh showed up looking like a rancher in his boots and jeans. A sizzling awareness of him gripped her. As usual, he began to help, working alongside her, as busy as she was until they finally sat to eat their own breakfast.

As they cleaned up the dining room and kitchen, the doorbell rang. "That's probably Lamont. I'll bring him in to meet you."

"This should be interesting," Josh stated.

When she opened the door, Lamont stepped inside, stamping his feet on the mat. He shrugged off his coat, removed his hat and gloves and crossed the hall to hang them on a coatrack that stood in the corner. He raked his fingers through his straight blond hair.

"The weather is better, but it's still cold and nasty out there. How are you doing?"

"Fine, considering we've been snowbound."

"It's slick out there, and we have deep drifts in spots. I have chains on my tires. I wanted to get here before other people get on the streets. Is Edwin around?"

"He's upstairs in his suite. But first, come meet one of the guests who's been very helpful since my brother and sister aren't here." She led him to the kitchen.

Josh put the lid on the coffeepot and turned when they entered, crossing the room to meet them.

"Josh, this is Lamont Nealey. Lamont, meet Josh Calhoun," she said, looking at the two together. Josh, with his brown hair, darker skin and dark eyes, looked more dynamic, but perhaps she thought that because she knew the personalities of both men. Lamont's paler skin was a reflection of his time spent indoors. He was seldom out, and as far as she knew, he did little physical exercise. He didn't convey the take-charge personality that Josh did, nor did he flirt. He was friendly, cooperative, intelligent and helpful about her bookkeeping, answering her questions when she had any. Lamont was absolutely reliable and he was hometown born and raised, just as she was. He was quiet, but she enjoyed the quiet, just as she had always enjoyed knowing Lamont.

"Can you sit and join us a minute?" Josh asked.

"I'd like to, but I better find Edwin. You're a little out of the way in Beckett, aren't you? I thought you lived in Dallas. I've seen your name in Texas magazines."

"I have a home in Dallas. I flew in here to see Jim Lee Hearne about buying a horse, and by the time we were through talking, it was all the cabbie could do to drive me back into town. The roads were closed and I had to stay in Beckett, which has proven to be nice."

"Good. Beckett is a very nice town." Lamont glanced at his watch.

"Well, it was nice to meet you, and I'm glad you found a place to stay. This has been a beast of a late snowstorm and I hope the last one for this year."

"It was nice to meet you, too, Lamont. I've heard a lot about you," Josh said as Lamont and Abby started toward the door.

"I hope it was all good," Lamont said, smiling and turning to look at Abby before he continued out of the room with her. She walked beside him up the stairs.

"I'm glad to see this weather clear," he said, "but it gave me a chance to get a lot of tax work done while people couldn't come to the office. It was a good time for uninterrupted work. You don't need to come up with me, Abby. Edwin is expecting me, and we'll be going over his taxes. I'll let you know when I'm leaving."

"Sure, Lamont," she said, pausing at the landing halfway up. She turned and walked back down to find Josh standing at the end of the hall, watching her.

A rising panic gripped her. Lamont had paled in so many ways next to Josh. Lamont was wrapped up in himself, his job, his own little world to an extent she had never noticed before. Perhaps it was just because it was tax season. This time of year, he always became tense, buried in work and preoccupied. He hadn't done the things Josh would have—asked if she needed help, inquired about when her brother and sister would return. Lamont was earnest, serious and reliable, and that had been enough to suit her until Josh crossed her path. How big a disaster was Josh turning out to be in her life? And was she contributing to it by agreeing to go to New York with him? Lamont would think she'd lost her wits or was sleeping with Josh, but she was glad she had suggested to Lamont they date other people.

Josh came forward with his phone in his hand. "The roads are being cleared, but Beckett isn't on a main highway, so it'll probably be tomorrow before I can get out of here."

She felt an emptiness over the thought of Josh leaving. He made his presence felt. She thought of her father and how charming he could be with the same type of personality, dynamic, charismatic, winning friends, yet so unreliable. He had broken her mother's heart, never being faithful, never able to stop charming everyone he came in contact with. She had always vowed she wanted the man in her life to be dependable, reliable, steady, settled—like Lamont. Josh was a man like her father, and she was following in her mother's footsteps and should stop right now. Josh had helped her partly to be nice, but also to keep busy, and she was the only single woman around. He had turned on the charm and been helpful, but if she had shown up in his hometown, he would never have looked twice at her. She should back out of the New York trip, tell Josh goodbye and start trying to forget him. She suspected she wasn't going to forget him for a long time.

New York with Josh—letting him take her out and show her some of the things she had never dreamed of seeing in person—sounded so exciting. She sighed with indecision. She should back out, but she wanted to go. Josh would make sure she had a good time. And he was right—this would be a once-in-a-lifetime weekend.

"That's great," she said quietly. "I know you want to get home."

He pulled out his phone. "I need your cell number— tell me and I'll put it in my phone right now."

With a heavy heart, she watched him enter her number. Then she turned. "I better get back to the kitchen."

"I'll help you with the chores and we'll be through in no time."

"You're a guest, remember? You don't have to work constantly."

"Beats sitting still and doing nothing, and I've got my emails caught up and have taken care of all my business that I can from here. This weekend makes up for the past week," he said as they walked to the kitchen.

It was an hour later, as they had the table set for lunch, that Lamont appeared. "Am I interrupting?" he asked, frowning as he stared at Josh.

"No, not at all," Josh replied. He had been helping Abby put two trays of dessert into the refrigerator. He stepped away. "Did you finish with Mr. Hickman?" she asked while Lamont stood watching them.

"For now. He has some forms to fill out. I better get home and back to figuring taxes. This is my busiest time."

"I think right now it's Abby's busiest time," Josh remarked.

"Yes, I suppose. Good to have met you," Lamont said abruptly. As he walked out of the kitchen, Abby went with him to the front door.

"That Calhoun fellow is worth a billion," Lamont said while he shrugged into his coat. "I'd think he could have found somewhere else to stay. What in the world is he doing in Beckett? I know what he said, but why would he want a horse?"

"He's also a rancher."

Lamont glanced away. "Can you feed all the people you have here?"

"Yes. I couldn't if this storm lasted through today,

but someone can get me groceries today, or I can walk over there myself and carry some groceries back."

"Want me to send Tommy over? He cleared my driveway this morning. He could get your groceries."

"Thanks anyway. I'll get along, and I can probably get out tomorrow."

"If that Calhoun fellow is helping you out here, it's because he wants on your good side for some reason—to keep whatever room you have him in. He didn't become a billionaire by being nice. You should stay away from him."

"Being rich doesn't rule out being nice. He's been very helpful." She crossed her arms over her chest. "He asked me if you and I have ever talked about marriage."

"That's a personal question to ask you and none of his business," Lamont said, frowning even more. "Is he the reason for your call about wanting to go out with other people?"

"I just think maybe we'd both be better off if we see others at least a bit."

"We'll talk about it again after tax season," Lamont said. "Right now I've got all I can deal with."

"I know you do," she said, thinking how different Josh's remarks would be if she had a similar conversation with him. He would flirt, make light of the questions and ask more about her situation. She knew it wasn't fair to compare Lamont with Josh, but it was impossible to avoid noticing differences.

"Lamont, Josh has asked me to go to New York this weekend. He has a new hotel opening he wants to attend. It's just the weekend to see the sights, sort of a thank-you for taking him in out of the storm."

Lamont narrowed his eyes at her. "So that's why you called. You want to date Josh Calhoun."

"No. When I called, he hadn't asked me to go to New York. Being free to date others is something I've been thinking about and want to do. It may be better for both of us."

"It may be at that. I'm shocked if you're going out of town for a weekend with him, but that will make it clear to everyone in Beckett that we aren't exclusive."

The phone rang, and she pulled it from her pocket. "Excuse me, Lamont."

"You take your call. I've got to get back to work. I don't know when I'll see you again," he said and left.

She answered her phone and heard her brother's voice. While she talked and learned both her brother and sister might get home late that night, she stood by the window to watch Lamont get into his car and drive slowly away. She was certain he had already forgotten all about her and was thinking about taxes. How would Lamont react if she told him Josh had kissed her in the shadow of the trees under a full moon? Lamont didn't believe the old legend for one second. Twice he had been with her and others when the heart-shaped shadow had occurred, but he had merely shaken his head and said it was a silly story.

She finished the call with her brother and returned to the kitchen to find Josh making coffee.

"You're getting so you can do this all by yourself," she said, amused as she watched him.

"Has Lamont gone?"

"Yes. He's preoccupied when it's tax season."

"I've called Benny to come pick me up around three," Josh said, turning to her as soon as he finished with the coffee. "I've talked to my pilot. The weather is clear, so I can get home today."

"So you'll be gone today for sure."

"Yes, I will," he said, walking closer to her. "Miss me?"

"Of course, I'm going to miss you terribly—you're better help than my siblings." Her voice changed and became sultry as she ran her finger across his shoulder, feeling his soft brown sweater over hard muscles. "You're definitely better looking and more fun."

His dark eyes flickered. "Now I don't want to go," he said, sliding his arms around her.

Smiling, she pushed his arms away. "You bring that out in me. Maybe I've been cooped up too long."

"The weekend is coming, and it'll be fun. Abby, I don't know if you go out to eat much in Beckett—"

Smiling, she shook her head. "No, I don't. Sometimes the family drives to a chicken place along one of the county roads, and after church sometimes we'll eat at the hotel downtown, but not often. Actually, the food is better here or at Mom's."

"Do you and Lamont go out to dinner?"

"We rarely ever have. If we're going to something— a movie we want to see—we usually eat separately at home first and then go. It's easier."

"When you were in school, didn't boys besides Lamont ask you out?"

"Yes, but I really never had much fun with any of them, and we didn't like the same things. I don't know that I have so much fun with Lamont, but we do like the same things, so that works out. And Lamont doesn't make demands on me or my time."

"It surprises me that you didn't find anyone you had fun with," Josh said.

"Maybe a couple, but I'm wrapped up in my family, and I didn't go to college and have that chance to meet more people my age. Besides, in high school, I wasn't ready for sex with those guys, and I've been told more than once or twice that I'm very cold."

"That speaks volumes about them," Josh said.

She nodded. "And the few times I've gone out with someone besides Lamont, I think my family might have been a bit much for them. My relatives either live here or right next door. They're a huge part of my life."

"You said Lamont doesn't have a lot of family. He can deal with yours?"

"He just stays away. Like I said, we don't go out a lot."

"And you don't want to leave Beckett?"

"Oh, no. This is my home, my life, my livelihood. My family is here, which is the most important thing. Why would I want to leave Beckett?"

Josh smiled. "I can think of a few reasons why you might want to live elsewhere. Not getting snowbound, for one."

She could hear the laughter in his voice. "You don't understand because you're a cosmopolitan, sophisticated world traveler. You just can't imagine the satisfaction I find in my work and this town and the friends I have."

He seemed to take that in. "I'll bet I'm not the first single guy who has stayed here and wanted to take you out."

"You're just the first one I couldn't resist," she said as he started to put the dishes on a shelf. When he set them back on the counter and turned to look at her, she shrugged. "That's just a fact. Don't let it go to your head."

"It just went somewhere else," he said, crossing the room to her. "I find that a very candid, interesting statement." As he placed his hands on her waist, his gaze traveled over her features with curiosity in his dark eyes. "I can't wait for the weekend. I want to see if you can resist me then."

"This better be just a friendly, fun trip."

"I intend it to be," he said. "When I asked about eating out in Beckett, I had a purpose. In case you don't feel you have a dress for New York, when we arrive, I'll take you to a shop and you can get a dress to wear that night when we go out to dinner."

"You don't have to buy me a dress," she said, smiling at him.

"Of course I don't have to. I want to. You select it or I will, but you'll get a new dress, I promise you. Now I hear people coming."

"Probably looking for me," she said, turning to go into the hall, trying to even imagine herself in a fancy dress, let alone at a fancy New York City restaurant.

At two-thirty in the afternoon, Abby sat at the desk in her room. She heard the scrape of boot heels on the floor, and she glimpsed Josh enter and cross the room he had rented for his stay. He glanced through the open door and saw her. "Can I come in?"

"Sure. I'm working on records and very glad for an interruption."

"My plane is waiting. I'll check out and be on my way. Do you have enough help for dinner tonight?"

"Sure," she answered, wishing she didn't feel a loss, but certain she'd get over it soon. "Nearly everyone has checked out. One family will still be here tonight, plus Mr. Hickman."

"Good. You'll have a quiet night. I have to pack my things. I'll tell you when I'm ready to check out."

She nodded, feeling an emptiness and hating to see

him go. She couldn't recall feeling the same way about anyone who had ever stayed at the inn. Ideally by tomorrow she wouldn't feel this way. Josh hadn't been in her life long enough to make any giant difference. As quickly as the thought came, she considered the trip to New York. That trip might make a giant difference.

Once again, common sense said to back out of going with him. It wasn't like anything she had ever done in her life. She had to tell her family, and she suspected all of them would try to talk her out of going. As small a town as Beckett was, everyone knew what everyone else was doing most of the time. Particularly if someone left town. Her absence would be conspicuous because of where she had gone and whom she had gone with. She knew she'd better break the news to her mother and grandmother first.

Then again, would Josh really come back to get her on Friday and take her to New York?

For the first time, she realized that once he returned home to the world he was accustomed to, he might back out of the trip. With a sigh, she bent over the books open in front of her and tried to concentrate.

It was only a few minutes until he knocked again. "Hate to interrupt you, but I'm ready to check out."

Abby stood, a hollow feeling in her chest. "Since you worked constantly, I'm not charging you for your stay. You've earned it totally, and I really appreciate what you did."

He smiled and dropped the bag he carried, walking closer. "I didn't do that much, and I want to pay, so just give me the bill. C'mon, I insist."

"Josh, this is ridiculous when you worked the whole time."

"No, it's not. Now that's settled, there's something

else—I'll call you about when I'll be back Friday to get you. I'll bring you home Sunday—or Monday. I suspect you'll get to the city and decide you want to stay maybe one more night."

"I don't think so. I'm beginning to wonder about going, and I imagine you are, too. Here's your chance—I'll let you off the hook if you want. I will understand absolutely."

"No way. I'm looking forward to it and have already started making plans." He walked up to her and placed his hands on her waist. "I'm not backing out and I don't want you to, either. I'm going to do everything I can to see to it that you have a great time and don't regret going. Now, until Friday," he said and paused.

He slid an arm around her waist and drew her against him as he leaned close to kiss her. Without hesitation, she wrapped her arms around his waist and held him tightly, pressing against his solid length. She kissed him as if she would never see him again.

His arms tightened and he leaned over her, kissing her until all thought stopped. The only awareness she had was of Josh's kisses. Her heartbeat raced and desire enveloped her, making her tremble and want so much more with him. She wished she could keep him from going for just a while longer.

He raised his head slightly. "I won't ever forget this time here."

"Yes, you will, but that's nice to say," she whispered and stepped away from him.

"I'll call you about arrangements Friday."

She nodded. "Ready to go?"

"Sure," he said, his dark eyes intent on her. He walked with her to the front desk.

"I feel ridiculous charging you," she said.

"Go ahead. I meant it. Besides, I didn't really do that much or work that hard."

"We won't keep arguing that one," she said, typing in the figures, showing him the amount and printing out his bill after he had paid. "Here you are," she said. "Paid in full."

He smiled. "I'll call."

She walked around the counter to go with him to the door. The cab waited at the foot of the porch steps, and she waved at the driver. "Have a good flight, Josh."

"Bye, Abby," he said and hurried to climb into the cab. He waved again as they drove away. She had a sinking feeling that she had seen the last of him in spite of all his talk about going to New York. When she walked back inside, she met Mr. Hickman, who had just come from the dining room.

"Josh just left. He's invited me to go to New York with him this weekend for a new hotel opening he wants to attend."

"I hope you're going."

"I am, because it may be the only time I'll ever see New York."

"I hope you have a better reason than that. He's a special fellow, Abby."

"Yes, he is. I've told Lamont we ought to go out with other people for a while because we've never done that since high school."

"I think that's an excellent idea. Marriage for someone like you would be a lifetime bond. You should meet others now, while you're young. I'm glad Josh was snowbound here. Very glad, since I get a fishing trip out of his stay," he said, smiling. "You go to New York and have the time of your life."

"Mr. Hickman, I'm going to Mom's house. While

I'm gone, I'm closing the front desk. Will you be downstairs?"

"Yes. I'll watch. If anyone comes in, I'll see what they want, and I can call you."

"I won't be gone long. Everyone has checked out except the Taylors, who aren't leaving until tomorrow, so it should be very quiet. Thanks for sitting here. I'll be home soon."

"Don't rush," Mr. Hickman said as she walked away to get her coat and gloves.

She needed to tell her mother about New York, even though she would believe it when it happened. She knew Josh would be back for Mr. Hickman's fishing trip, but would Josh really come back this Friday for her?

"Thanks for picking me up, Benny," Josh said as the cab pulled away from the curb, snow crunching beneath the tires.

"It's been a slow day. A lot of people are still not getting out because that snow is deep and the town's streets are covered and slick. How'd it go at the inn?"

"Great. Abby is nice, and it's been a good place to stay. The food is the best," he said, realizing it had been. "Abby is a good cook." He thought about her biscuits, which were the lightest he had ever eaten. Until Abby, he'd thought his cook and his mother made the best possible. Also, Abby's salmon cakes would be worth driving from Dallas back to Beckett.

"We have a town picnic in the summer. People come from all around, and whatever Abby cooks and brings is gone first," Benny said. "She's even better than her grandmother was when she ran the inn, and that's saying a lot."

Josh nodded. "Benny, have you ever thought of moving away from Beckett?"

"Move out of Beckett? Nah, I don't think so."

"Abby mentioned that you've worked in construction. I can get you on a construction crew. It would mean moving, though. Same thing with my brother, who has an energy business in Dallas. He might have a place for you in the oil field if you want to go talk to him."

"That's nice, thanks. I'll take his name. I've never even thought about moving away from here."

"It's still in Texas," Josh said, smiling as Benny glanced at him in the rearview mirror and gave him a thumbs-up.

"That's important. Doubt if my wife would leave Texas."

"When I get out, I'll give you my business card, and I'll put his name and number on it," he said, writing Jake's name on the back of a card.

"That's great. Thanks."

"Sure. You helped me." As they left the last houses in Beckett, Josh looked at the white world stretching all around him.

He listened to Benny talking, but his mind was on what he needed to do before the weekend trip to New York. He was amazed Abby had agreed to go with him, but glad. After meeting Lamont, he didn't think she would spend ten seconds worrying about Lamont's reaction to her going to New York with another man.

Sending a text to his secretary, Josh asked her to find the best possible French restaurant in New York and make reservations for two for Friday night. He called a private club he belonged to and made reservations for Saturday night.

He couldn't wait for Friday. He wanted Abby to have

the time of her life, and he wanted her in his arms, in his bed, to make love to her for hours. Was it possible for that to happen?

Next door, Abby found her mother in the kitchen putting a meat loaf in the oven.

"Can't I help with anything?" Abby asked, pouring herself a cup of coffee and sitting at the table.

"Just sit. I imagine you've been worked to pieces the past few days with the inn overflowing."

"I had a lot of help from one of the guests. I'll be glad to help you now."

"No, I'm almost ready for a break. I'll get some tea and sit with you. Grandma is napping, and if she doesn't get up in a little while, I'll wake her, because she'll want to see you while you're here. She said you might know who shoveled our drive and porch steps this morning."

Surprised, Abby looked out the window. "Mom, that was probably my guest. He was very helpful all the time he was here."

"That was really nice. Did he know I'm your mom?"

"Yes. And he probably knew you needed your drive cleared. You don't have any customers to get their hair or nails done today?"

"Heavens, no. Everyone canceled when snow began to fall a few days ago. I'm glad they did, because I've enjoyed the lull."

Having had a break, maybe her mother wouldn't mind covering for her at the inn while she was in New York. "Mom, can you cover for me this weekend? Justin and Arden said they can help if they get home by then."

"Sure, I'll cover. What's going on? Lamont is in tax season, so you're not doing anything with him."

"No, I'm not. Besides, I've talked to Lamont, and we're going to date other people for a while."

"That's a big change in your life," her mother said, her eyebrows arching in surprise. "What are you doing this weekend that I need to cover for you?"

"Josh Calhoun—he's the one who helped and shoveled the drives—has invited me to go out this weekend. Josh is from Dallas and Verity. He has his own hotel business with the headquarters in Dallas. Mom, he asked me to go with him to a new hotel he's opening this Friday in New York, and I said I would."

"New York City? My, oh, my," she said, her blue eyes widening. "Are you in love with him?"

"No, but I like being with him. I think part of it is, he feels sorry for me because I've never been out of Texas. And part of it is gratitude because I let him stay at the inn so he could get out of the blizzard."

"A trip to New York. That's a big deal. He must be important. I just don't want you hurt. He sounds a bit like your father, except wealthier."

Abby smiled. "I'll take care, but it's something I may never have a chance to do again. He's very nice. He's coming back in April or May and taking Edwin Hickman fishing in Colorado."

"I can't imagine. Have you checked on his background?"

"Yes, and Mr. Hickman has. He owns Calhoun Hotels and he's a rancher. He said I could call the sheriff of Verity, Texas, if I want a reference, because he's known him all his life."

Her mother gazed at her for a few moments and then nodded. "You're young, but a grown, intelligent woman, so go and have a wonderful time. Call me, will you?"

"I will. And I'll be careful. I'll tell Grandma about the trip."

"Let me tell her gently. I don't want her to have a heart attack."

"You're kidding me, aren't you? I hate to leave without saying hello to Grandma, but I'd better get back to the inn."

"I'm glad you came over and told me. My friend Marilee goes to Dallas a lot. Care if I ask her if she knows who Josh Calhoun is?"

"Of course not. Ask any of your friends or customers," she said, getting her coat and pulling it on again. "He's nice, Mom."

"Just don't fall in love with him. Men who have private planes and hotel chains do not fall in love with inn owners from places like Beckett, Texas. It would be heartbreak."

"I know. I'm going to see New York while I have a chance. At least as much as you can see in the blink of an eye. We'll just have a full day on Saturday. Fly in on Friday and out on Sunday."

"That's long enough to fall in love. You take care of yourself."

They hugged lightly, and Abby jammed her cap over her ponytail and left, calling over her shoulder, "Tell Grandma hi for me."

She walked through new snow back to the inn, thinking about what she would pack to wear for a weekend in New York City. Her wardrobe was simple.

By eight that evening, the only guests watched a movie and Mr. Hickman had disappeared upstairs, so she had the first chance to look at her clothes and lay things out to pack, aware that she might have to put them all back if Josh canceled.

Shortly after ten that night, Josh called, and they talked on the phone until past midnight. After the connection was broken, she stared at the phone, still wondering if she would regret going with him for the weekend, if her mother was right about it leading to heartbreak.

She couldn't back out. This trip to New York might be the one time in her life that she could step out and do something exciting, unforgettable, something she had never expected to do.

She was surprised that Josh had called and that they'd talked so long. Sure, they'd talked for hours at a time when he had been here, but he had been snow-bound. Now he was in Dallas, home where his friends lived, where he knew lots of people, so it surprised her that he called at all.

Would she come back from New York in love with him? He wasn't going to make any commitment—he had made that more than clear. And soon, he would want her in his bed, although she had told him plainly to not expect that.

What did he look forward to? Seduction? Maybe just a fun weekend together. She knew better than that, but she had warned him that was all she intended to do. Now she just had to resist him.

Six

At noon Wednesday when Josh walked into a restaurant for lunch, Lindsay and Jake were already waiting. He shook hands with Jake and hugged Lindsay. "Hey, this is good. Lindsay, you should come to Dallas more often."

"Heaven forbid," she said, smiling at him. "I come only when I absolutely have to." She turned to Jake. "You should have brought Madison."

"She had an appointment with a gallery in Fort Worth, and she's having lunch with the owner, so business first. Mike has an excuse for not making the Calhoun sibling lunch because of his honeymoon. Let's get our table."

After they were seated and had ordered, Jake turned to Josh. "You were snowbound for the weekend in some little town. I'll bet you went stir-crazy."

"Did you have trouble finding a place to stay?" Lindsay asked.

"Yes, I did. I was afraid I'd have to sleep in the park in Beckett. A very nice B and B owner let me have the front room of her personal suite—"

"Let me guess," Jake said. "She's single."

"As a matter of fact, she is. She had four others who were on the floor or sofas. That inn was packed. Be glad the storm veered north."

"We got a few flurries, some sleet and then rain," Lindsay said, "but nothing that would strand anyone, thank goodness. We've already had enough of that. I'm ready for spring."

"How're the horses?" Josh asked her.

"Beautiful. You'll have to see my new foal. He's perfect."

"Here comes the picture of her baby," Jake teased.

Lindsay stuck her tongue out at him as she pulled out her phone and handed it to Josh. "How's that? Isn't he adorable?"

"He is adorable," Josh agreed, smiling as he handed her phone back. The waiter came with their orders and placed burgers in front of Jake and Josh, while Lindsay had a tossed salad.

Jake sipped a tall glass of iced tea. "If Mike and Savannah get back this week, Madison and I'll have everybody for dinner Saturday night—how'll that work with both of you?"

"I'm out," Josh said instantly.

"I can't, either. I've already made arrangements to go to Austin to a horse sale this weekend," Lindsay said.

"And I'm going to a hotel opening in New York."

Jake turned to look at Josh. "You don't go to hotel openings. Not in a long, long time. In New York?"

"I'm going to this one," Josh said, looking at Jake's disbelieving brown eyes.

"So you're taking someone, is my guess. I'll bet it's someone who was staying at that B and B. Give you three days shut up somewhere if there is a single woman who is appealing, you'll have a date with her, although someone from Beckett, Texas, isn't your style."

"So it's one of the guests?" Lindsay asked, her blue eyes twinkling.

"You're so far off."

"I don't think I am. I'll buy lunch for us all if I'm wrong."

Josh grinned. "Okay. I'm taking the owner of the B and B."

"You wasted no time this past weekend," Jake said. "She's going with you to New York? I won't say what I'm thinking in front of Lindsay's delicate ears, but that's fast work."

Lindsay laughed with Josh. "Lindsay spends every day working alongside those cowboys at her ranch. There isn't anything Lindsay's delicate ears haven't heard," Josh said.

"You're right," Lindsay said, "but I don't have to listen to my brothers' raunchy remarks. So, Jake, can you have the dinner for Mike another time, please?"

"Sure. Mike and Savannah aren't due back from their honeymoon for a while anyway. Scotty is doing fine, though I'm sure he misses them. He's with his sitter, and Mom and Dad visited yesterday"

"Scotty is coming to my house soon to stay a week," Lindsay said. "We'll have a blast."

"Yes, you will. Scotty loves his aunt Lindsay. And vice versa. You're good with horses and little kids," Jake said.

"Thank you," she said, smiling at him.

Jake looked at Josh again. "So tell us about the latest

love in your life—she owns a bed-and-breakfast inn—
what else? We never meet these women of yours, so I
don't expect to meet this one."

"You'll probably never meet her," Josh said. "This
is just a weekend trip. She's never been out of Texas so
I'm taking her to New York."

Jake and Lindsay both laughed. "This doesn't sound
like our cynical, worldly brother's type of lady," Jake
observed. "Never flown and never out of Texas? What
does she do in her spare moments?"

"I don't think she has many. Her life is tied up with
her family—a sister, a brother, her mother, her two
great-aunts, her grandmother—and running the inn."

"You met all these people at the B and B?" Lindsay asked.

"No, none of the above. All were snowed in or
snowed out and couldn't get back home. The elderly
aunts live in the B and B along with an elderly gentle-
man. You'll find out anyway, so I might as well tell you
that I'm taking him fishing in a few weeks," Josh said.

Jake choked on his tea and set down his glass to stare
at Josh. "I don't think I heard right."

"You heard right, and it's not that big a deal. You can
come along if you want. I'm flying him to Colorado.
He reminds me of Granddad."

"No kidding," Jake said, staring at Josh.

"Is the B and B owner going with you?" Lindsay
asked, and both of them stared at Josh.

"No, she isn't," Josh said, smiling at them. "She's
only going to New York this weekend. Lindsay, close
your mouth. You're staring."

"No more than Jake is," she said, exchanging a
glance with Jake.

"I'll be damned, you've fallen in love. I didn't think

that would happen for another ten years," Jake said while Lindsay continued to look wide-eyed at him.

"I have not fallen in love. Don't be ridiculous, either one of you. I just met her. She's nice and hasn't ever been anywhere, and elderly Edwin Hickman, who lives at the inn, loves fishing, so I asked him to go fishing. I don't know why I'm explaining this to the two of you. Suffice it to say, I'm being a nice guy."

"I'll be damned," Jake said again. "You're a nice guy, but in a different way. I can't recall you taking a senior fishing before. I can't believe it when I hear you say it."

"Don't sound like I'm an ogre. It just worked out that way. You plan your dinner after Mike gets back. No telling when that will be."

"I will, and I'll let you know."

"I think something happened to you out there in the snow in that blizzard," Lindsay said. "Josh, this is so totally unlike you that I'm like Jake—I can't believe what I hear you say. As much fun as all this is, I have to go because I have a dental appointment." She stood. "Josh, I've just seen a whole new side of you that I've never seen before. It's very nice of you to take the elderly man on a fishing trip and your lady friend who has never flown, never been out of Texas, to New York. Remind me to call you next time I need some help birthing a calf or some such."

"Forget it, Lindsay," Josh said. "You can do that blindfolded."

"Well, I'm impressed with my big brother and these charitable trips."

"He gets a pat on the back," Jake said.

"Enough of you two. I'll think twice before we have the next lunch."

"No, you won't," Lindsay said as her brothers stood.

She hugged them briefly. "See you both soon." She left, her blond hair swinging with each step as they sat again.

"We didn't hear about her latest fight with Tony Milan," Josh said.

"Maybe those two have let up a bit."

"Oh, yeah," Josh said, "and the sky is pink today. They keep the old Calhoun-Milan feud alive and well."

"Madison and I have done our part to end it," Jake said, glancing at his watch. "I've got to go, too. I'll get the check today."

"Thanks. Let me know about dinner."

"Sure. Have a great time in New York. She may be terrified of the big city."

"I don't think she'll be terrified, but she may not like it. It's a far cry from Beckett."

"I don't even know Beckett. It must be smaller than Verity," Jake said as they walked out of the restaurant.

"I'm sure it is. One small hotel and the bed-and-breakfast—that was it. No motels. It's not right on the highway, and my pilot and I were lucky they had a runway and a place to land—I'm guessing it's for the ranchers out in that area. Good to see you," he said, unlocking his car and climbing inside to drive to his office.

As he sat behind his desk, he shoved aside a stack of papers to read later. Restless, filled with an uncustomary lack of interest in business, he thought about the ranch and the possibilities of taking a couple of weeks off soon and staying there. He had great executives who could run the company, including an executive vice president who could take charge and wouldn't need his help or direction.

Was this corporate world really what he wanted to continue to do? Was he missing life as Abby had said? No one had ever told him that before, and he wouldn't have listened to most anyone else. In addition to the New York trip, he would like to take her to the ranch, because that was what he really considered his home.

The moment he thought of Abby with him at his ranch, he wanted to do that soon. Would she like the ranch? He turned to look out the window at other buildings in downtown Dallas, but he was seeing Abby. He wanted to be with her, and he wished the weekend would arrive. He turned back to his computer to look up a number and make a call to a dress shop in New York. After he hung up, he called Abby and talked for twenty minutes until she had a guest needing her attention and had to go.

She was his total opposite—small-town, wrapped up in her family and where she'd grown up, very simple tastes and wants, yet he couldn't get her out of his thoughts. Maybe after this weekend when he would see her in his world, he could. He thought about her in New York with her ponytail hairdo, her slacks and plain shirts buttoned to her chin—would she want him to take her home early?

He couldn't imagine that she would really interest him long. He wouldn't be surprised if she backed out of going before the weekend came.

Continuing to be surprised by the fact that he wanted to take Abby to New York, he had to admit his brother and sister were right—that was unlike him. At least in some ways. But when he thought about their kiss in the heart-shaped shadow in the snow, mere memories made him hot with desire. No woman's kisses had ever affected him the way Abby's had.

What had started as a fun, lighthearted, meaningless kiss had shaken him and changed his views of her forever. He couldn't imagine ever forgetting her. How

long was that kiss going to be an influence in his life?
Would he get her out of his system in New York? Just
thinking about her made him want to talk to her and be
with her. He picked up his phone to call her again, saw
the stack of mail in front of him and resolved to wait
until night to call her.

He pulled the stack in front of him to go through
it, trying to get Abby out of his thoughts and get work
done.

During their last phone call, they had agreed she
would meet him Friday at Beckett's small airport that
consisted only of a tiny office, one small hangar and
runways that were too short for commercial jets. When
she arrived and walked toward the office, Josh came
out to meet her.

The minute she saw him, Abby's heart missed a beat.
All her doubts about going with him fell away. She became slightly self-conscious as wind blew a few ten-
drils of her hair across her cheek.

For the flight to Dallas and then New York, she had
dressed in navy slacks, a new pale-blue button-down
long-sleeve shirt with a collar and a light jacket, and
she had let down her hair. She was relieved to see Josh
dressed as casually in chinos and a navy sweater and
boots.

"Hi," he said. "I'm glad to see you."

"Hi, Josh. I'm still torn between wondering what I'm
doing going to New York and anticipating seeing you
and this trip. This is the most exciting thing in my life."

"More exciting than when we kissed in the heart-
shaped shadow?" he asked, a slight smile lifting one
corner of his mouth.

Startled, she blinked. "No, maybe not," she answered

truthfully. His smile vanished as his brown eyes darkened and his gaze lowered to her mouth.

"With an answer like that, what I'd like to do is take you home with me for the weekend," he said in a deeper voice.

She smiled again as she shook her head. "I don't believe so. That isn't what I agreed to do."

"New York it is. Let's board." As Josh took her arm, he smiled. "You look fantastic. I've never seen you with your hair down."

Keeping the thought to herself that he looked fantastic, too, she smiled. "Thank you. I'm glad you like it. It's naturally curly and a little difficult to manage."

"If you need to get it done in New York, I'll tell you where to go and you can use my credit card. It'll save you time for sightseeing and being with me."

She laughed. "I'll keep that in mind. I do my own hair except for haircuts. We have a shop in Beckett."

"You might like getting it done in New York. It'll be something else to tell your family you did."

As they boarded the plane, he motioned to her. "Sit by a window. You've never flown, and you'll like looking out. It's a sunny day between here and Dallas, so you'll have a view."

"I'm excited."

He smiled and took her hand. "I am, too, but not over the view of Texas. I'd rather you'd be excited for another reason, too. I've missed you, and I'm looking forward to this."

"Everything this weekend except you will be a first for me," she said, barely aware of what she told him, as her attention was on his hand holding hers. His hand was well-shaped, warm, callused in places, and though his touch was light, it sent a sizzling awareness of the physical contact.

"That's an interesting statement I've never heard from someone out with me before. So your family knows you're going with me?"

"Oh, yes. Even Grandma, who was reassured by Mr. Hickman that you're an okay guy and I'll be safe and have a good time. You better live up to all their descriptions and promises."

"Actually, I heard from Edwin. He called me. He didn't threaten me, but he clearly indicated he held me responsible for you. He told me that he was delighted I am taking you to New York and he knew you would have a wonderful, safe time."

"If that's what he said, then he certainly didn't threaten you, but I'm astounded he called you."

"It was a threat to see to it you have a good time and get home safely. A very subtle one, and I think you have a substitute grandfather."

They taxied to the end of the runway and in minutes were clear for takeoff. She turned to gaze out the window in fascination until Beckett was behind them.

"That was a thrill," she said.

He smiled. "I'm glad it's good weather and you can see for miles, even if all you're seeing now is mesquite, fields of grass or just bare ground and a rare stream."

"I can't believe this day is happening."

"It's happening, and I'm looking forward to going out tonight. This afternoon I'll have a limo that will take you to the dress shop. Get a dress for tonight and one for tomorrow night."

"Now it's two dresses you want to buy. That's a bit much."

"No, it's not. Stop worrying about something that I want to do. Tonight we'll go to a French restaurant."

"That sounds fabulous," she said.

"I think you look fabulous, and my after-dinner plans sound fabulous to me. A little dancing, a few kisses—you think I haven't been waiting for this weekend to come?"

"That's why I don't want you to buy dresses—I don't care to be obligated to you or anyone else except my family. Even my family, now that I'm an adult."

"You're free of any and all obligations," he said, his eyes twinkling. "I just hope you want a few kisses, too. That's the special part of the evening and has nothing to do with obligations and everything to do with desire."

"When you put it that way, it does sound like something to look forward to," she said in a sultry, breathless voice, flirting with him and enjoying herself. She never had this kind of fun with Lamont—or reactions out of him. The minute she spoke, Josh's amusement vanished, and he studied her intently while his chest expanded as he drew a deep breath.

"We have to stay buckled in right now, but what I'd like to do is pick you up and move you over here," he replied.

She tingled. "You wicked man," she teased, fanning herself with her hand. "Now I'm all hot and bothered, and you haven't even touched me." She laughed. "Stop flirting, Josh, before one of us does unbuckle and ends up somewhere we shouldn't."

His dark eyes were intent as he leaned forward, holding her chin with his hand. "There's no harm in flirting. It's fun and I know you think so, too, because you can't resist doing it."

She smiled. "You might be right. It does make the

time pass. Anticipation is exciting," she whispered, looking at his mouth.

His hand slipped behind her head, and he pulled her closer as his mouth covered hers. His kiss was deep, sending waves of heat, stirring desire until she finally leaned away to look at him again.

"Slow down—we have a weekend and we just got off the ground," she said. Her voice was weak and did not hold a shred of conviction to her own ears.

He sat back. "We're going to have a great weekend."

"Did you have trouble clearing your calendar to go?"

"Nope, because it's the weekend. Have you had many people check in since I left?"

"Not at all," she answered, telling him about the past few days, sitting back and enjoying the flight. It seemed short until they landed in Dallas and left the plane to board a larger one that was far more luxurious. While she was fascinated with the takeoff and the sensation of their speed and the lift of the plane, it all paled next to her awareness of Josh, which was sharp and constant.

Their topics of conversation had a wide range, and she learned more about his relatives and ancestors, as imbedded in Texas history as her own family.

He had a flight attendant serve soft drinks and sandwiches for lunch, and finally the pilot announced they were approaching New York. She was breathless over the view as they came in, flying over water, and suddenly they were on the ground and the flight was over.

Josh had a limo waiting. A uniformed driver stood and smiled when they walked up.

All the way to the hotel, she was mesmerized by the sights and sounds. "Josh, this is fantastic—all the noise and traffic and buildings. I've seen pictures, but it's different in real life." She turned to look at him. He sat smiling, watching her, his long legs stretched out, crossed at the ankles.

"You've seen it so much, it means nothing to you."

"I'm having more fun watching you, and I'm glad you like everything. It's a fabulous city."

"More than fabulous—absolutely awesome, as my sister would say. I'm going to be such a tourist and take a million pictures."

"I think I'll have to take a few pictures myself, but mine won't be of the city, except as a background for you."

"I might not want to go home."

He grinned. "Let me know and I'll see how long we can stay."

"You know I'm kidding. We go home Sunday," she said, turning back to look at everything, thankful she had accepted Josh's invitation. "I can't wait to get out there."

"I can't wait to get to the hotel room," he said in a husky voice that made her turn to look at him and forget the scenery.

"I won't ask why."

"You know exactly why, and I think you're a little eager yourself because your voice changes."

"I hoped you wouldn't notice, since I can't control that with you."

"I'm happier than ever you agreed to this weekend."

When the limo pulled to the front door of the hotel, she stepped out to walk into an elegant lobby with bouquets and sprays of flowers for the opening. People greeted Josh as he walked to the front desk.

On the top floor, they crossed a hall, and he unlocked a door. "This is your suite. Mine adjoins it, and the adjoining door locks on each side."

"Locked is fine." She smiled, looking at the beige and white decor. "This suite is beautiful, and so are the flowers," she said, glancing around a large living room. A bouquet of mixed fresh flowers and a clear-covered plate of cheeses, fruit and crackers were on a nearby table. There was a dining area and a spacious covered balcony with a high wall, potted plants and outdoor furniture. "Josh, this is breathtaking."

"Come see my suite. We'll have to go through the door from the hall."

She followed him down the short hall until he paused to unlock the door to his suite.

The living room was larger than hers, as was the dining area with luxurious furniture. He had a bigger balcony. Through an open door she saw a small kitchen, and she guessed a second open door led to a bedroom and bath. Another huge bouquet of mixed fresh flowers stood on the glass coffee table, and a covered spread of cheeses, fruit and crackers was on a table nearby. Champagne was on ice.

"This is beautiful, too," she said. He dropped his things and crossed the room to her to slip his arm around her waist.

"I've waited for this moment since I told you goodbye at the inn," he said, leaning down to kiss her. Both his arms banded her, holding her tightly pressed against him. His kiss spiraled to the center of her being, setting her ablaze as she slid her arms around his neck and clung tightly.

Was she speeding toward heartbreak, real heartbreak that might take a long time to get over and sour her relationship with dependable Lamont? The question was fleeting, dwindling to no importance because she wanted Josh's kisses. She wanted this exciting weekend that she otherwise might not ever have in her life. Just this once. Broken bones mended, so broken hearts must mend, too.

It could never be a relationship or much of anything except a few times out together, but she wanted what she could get. It might hurt later, but at least she wouldn't have giant regrets that she had let life pass her by.

Josh's kisses drove away all her inner worries and she yielded to him, returning his kiss as passionately as he kissed her. He was hard, strong, his lean body pressing against her.

He shifted, running his hand lightly along her throat, down over her breast, her waist and hip, lower along her thigh. He swung her up into his arms and carried her through the suite to place her on the bed.

He lowered himself, still holding his weight partially off her as he continued to kiss her until she pushed slightly and he raised his head.

She ran her finger along his clean-shaven jaw. "Watch out, Josh. The first thing you know, you're going to make that old Texas legend haunt you."

"At the moment, that doesn't sound like something to fear."

She smiled but changed the subject. "I think I have a dress appointment soon."

"You do, but I couldn't resist." He moved away and took her hand to help her up. "Want a moment to freshen up? We have about ten minutes before we have to leave."

"Yes, I do," she answered.

He nodded, falling into step beside her. "I'll come get you in ten minutes—how's that?" he said as he walked her back to her suite.

"See you then," she said, closing the door and turning to get ready for the afternoon, while her thoughts

were on the evening with Josh. Anticipation built with
every second—a dinner out in one of the most famous
cities in the world—a dinner with Josh. And dancing
with Josh, being in his arms. Her heart raced at the
thought, and eagerness enveloped her. Tonight would
be a night to remember forever.

Josh rode down in the elevator with her, taking her
arm lightly to walk to the front door. "I'll be here at the
hotel while you're gone. I have a couple of meetings.
The limo is yours for the afternoon. Just head back to
the hotel by five."

The driver, Reed, stood waiting, holding open the
door of the limo. She told Josh goodbye, climbed in and
glanced back to see Josh going in the front door of the
hotel. Everything in New York reminded her of the differences in their lives. She still was astounded he had
asked her up for the weekend. She couldn't imagine
why he was drawn to her at all. The women he dated,
she was certain, were sophisticated, like him, beautiful and accustomed to the same life as him. He was a
man of mystery in a lot of ways. She was as surprised
about his friendship with Mr. Hickman as she was by
his interest in her.

The limo halted in front of a shop, and Reed came
around to open the door for her.

"Thanks, Reed."

"Here's my number. Call me when you see you'll be
done and I'll come get you."

"Thank you," she said, pocketing the number and
turning to the boutique, feeling butterflies in her stomach. This was a far cry from Sandy Perkins's dress shop
in Beckett.

The friendly woman named Hilda, who had been

expecting her, soon ended the butterflies she felt. Instead, she was dazzled by the array of dresses Hilda brought out to show her and the treatment that made her feel like royalty.

She finally selected two dresses, which seemed incredibly extravagant, but she suspected if she didn't, Josh would return to the store with her and see to it that she purchased the second dress.

At one point, Hilda stood looking at Abby in a maroon dress. "That is perfect on you. If you would like to get your hair done this afternoon, there's a salon that I might get you in. It's on the next block, so you could walk. They're good and very nice."

Abby laughed. "Josh told you to ask me, didn't he?"

"No, actually, he didn't. And your hair looks nice. I just thought with your new dresses, you might like your hair done."

Abby thought a moment and nodded. "If they can take me, I have time, and it might be fun."

Hilda left and in minutes was back. "You're in luck. I've written everything down for you, and she can take you in an hour."

"Thank you. I'll be glad I did, I'm sure."

Her purchases made, she was so curious about the city, she asked Hilda to hold her packages while she walked down the street.

Sunshine spilled over buildings, traffic and pedestrians. A man passed on a skateboard, weaving in and out of traffic. Horns honked, and she enjoyed strolling along the avenue to the end of the block immersed in all the traffic, people hurrying past her, the sounds and sights that were so different from her world. She crossed the street to stroll along the other side, finally returning, gathering her packages and thanking Hilda. She went to the hair salon and in another hour called Reed and said she was ready to be picked up.

Back at the hotel, her eagerness grew steadily until it was only a minute before time for Josh to appear at her door.

She made one more check of how she looked. She had taken several pictures of her reflection in a mirror to send home and had already heard back from her mother and sister, who had seen the pictures. Her hair, parted in the middle, fell freely on both sides of her face in loose spirals. She had selected a simple sleeveless black dress that ended just above her knees deceptively modest neckline in front, but her back was left bare. She wore high-heeled black sandals and silver bangle earrings.

She heard Josh's light knock and picked up her black envelope purse. When she opened the door, her breath caught at the sight of Josh in his charcoal suit, red tie and white dress shirt; she also noticed his eyes widen with a look of surprise. "Do you want to come in?

"You look stunning," he said in a husky voice that indicated the reaction he was having. "Yeah, I want to come in, but if I do, we'll never get to the restaurant."

"Then I'm coming out," she said, grabbing a lightweight black blazer from a nearby chair and closing the door behind her.

The corner of his mouth lifted in amusement. "You don't want me to come in?"

"Right now, I want the French dinner more than a kiss."

"It wouldn't be just a kiss," he said, stepping into the elevator with her. People got on at the next floor, and they rode quietly until they got out in the lobby.

Reed and the limo waited, and soon they were driving through New York traffic as the sun slid behind tall buildings.

"So you like the dress I selected today? And thank you very much. It was fun and exciting and they were all very nice to me, which makes me wonder about your life and how many women you've sent to that store to get dresses. But it's none of my business, so you don't have to tell me."

"Actually, you're the first, but my mother has shopped there, and on a rare occasions when my sister is in New York for a horse show, she goes there. Hilda always helps Mom and Lindsay. " He glanced at her black dress. "You look fantastic."

"Thank you," she replied. "You don't have hotel business tonight?"

"No, I took care of everything that needed my involvement for the opening of the hotel. I'm free for the rest of the weekend, which will be devoted to entertaining you."

"That's very nice, but it doesn't seem to me that you're really very involved," she said.

"I'm involved all I care to be. Don't be concerned."

"Fine. You know your business, and I don't."

The restaurant was on the top floor of a tall building, and the view was spectacular. They sat by floor-to-ceiling windows in a dimly lit dining area with black linen tablecloths, red roses, and candles in hurricane globes centered on the tables. A string quartet played, and there was a small dance floor, but no one dancing yet.

"This is lovely, Josh."

"Yes, it is," he said, studying her and indicating he meant her and not the view outside or the elegant restaurant.

A waiter came, and Josh ordered champagne. After they were alone, he turned to her. "We'll celebrate."

"What could we possibly be celebrating? That you're no longer snowbound in Beckett? That we made a safe flight to New York? That we're out in New York tonight? I can't guess."

The waiter returned to show Josh the selection. He uncorked it, went through all the traditional procedures and finally poured a glass for her and then one for Josh and set the remaining champagne in the bottle in the stand.

When they were alone, Josh raised his glass. "Here's to your first trip to New York. May you have many more. May it be a happy, unforgettable visit, in your memory for years to come, and may you begin to see how happy you've made me that you came to New York."

"That's a nice toast, but you can't be serious. You're not going to want to remember this night with me for years. Or care if I do."

"Oh, yes, I'll remember. You're unique in my life. I don't know anyone else like you. And I really do want you to have a fun trip. This is my gratitude for rescuing me from the blizzard."

"As helpful and resourceful as you are, you would have managed quite well." She touched his champagne flute lightly with hers and sipped the golden, bubbly liquid, looking into his brown eyes over the rim. She had a running current of excitement with him, but it was even stronger tonight. She expected to dance with him and to kiss him, and that kept excitement churning. On top of being in New York, she was completely dazzled. She raised her glass.

"May you have a great opening of your newest hotel and not get stranded in any more blizzards."

"Thank you." They touched glasses again and sipped. "Do you know when your inn first opened?" he asked as he set his flute on the table.

"Only the year—1887—a very long time ago."

They talked as tossed greens on crystal plates were served. When she finished her dinner of creamed lobster and grilled asparagus, she placed her fork across her plate.

"Are you ready to dance?" he asked.

"I'd love to," she said as he came around to hold her chair. On the dance floor, he turned to take her into his arms. Her heart thudded while she followed his lead, dancing with him to the string quartet playing an old ballad.

She was intensely aware of him pressed against her, holding her close as they moved together. His hand was on her bare back, sending tingles all through her. As they danced, his hand trailed down to her waist, slowly, a light caress. She couldn't get her breath and thought about kisses later.

They danced well together—that much even she could tell. The string quartet finally played a fast song. As she danced around him, watching his moves, she was certain he would want to make love this weekend, and she had to make a decision.

Until this week, she wouldn't have given ten seconds of thought to such a choice; she would not have been interested. Now she thought about her future with Lamont or another man from Beckett, a routine, quiet life with little change from the life she had always known and perhaps little attention from the man she might someday marry—never the excitement she had with Josh.

She watched Josh dance, his dark eyes steadily on her while every move he made was sexy. She stopped worrying about it—a decision to make another time, not yet—and gave herself to enjoying dancing with him. So far the weekend had been like a dream. She was going to go home in love with Josh even though she knew it would never be returned and wouldn't work out regardless.

Seven

At one in the morning, after a stroll around Times Square with a mob of people, they finally headed back to the hotel.

"Want a nightcap, Josh?" Abby asked as she placed her purse and her jacket on a chair in her room. Watching her, he shed his suit jacket and removed his tie, unbuttoning the top buttons of his shirt.

"Yes," he said as he dropped his tie on the chair. "There should be a cold beer in that fridge in your kitchen. If you don't find what you want, we can call room service."

They walked into the kitchen, and she opened the small refrigerator. "I see grape soda pop, which will be fine for me," she said, getting the soda and the beer.

"It's a nice night. Want to sit on the balcony?" he asked.

"I'd love to turn out the lights and sit on the balcony and look at the city, which is absolutely fascinating."

"I'm glad you like the city, and I'll have to admit that I'm surprised. I thought you wouldn't care for it very much. Sort of 'I want to see, and now I can go home.'"

"Oh, no. I think I could spend the year here and not see all I want to see. As it is, we have a day, so let's go sit, and you tell me what we're going to do tomorrow."

He switched off lights, leaving on one small light above the kitchen counter. They walked through the suite. In the living area, he set down their drinks to unlock and open the sliding glass door. A breeze swept in from the balcony.

"This is a beautiful hotel," she said.

He turned to slip his arm around her. "I've waited all week for this moment," he said in a husky voice. "I've dreamed of holding you and kissing you, and I don't want to wait another minute." He leaned closer to kiss her, and she wrapped her arms around him tightly to press against him.

He kissed her with such hunger and desperation that she trembled. His hand drifted lightly down her back until he found the zipper at the waist of her backless dress and unfastened it slowly. His hand slipped beneath her dress, down over her bottom.

The intimate caress made her moan as she unfastened the buttons on his shirt. She wanted to touch him as he touched her, to slide her hands over him and excite him as he did her.

He leaned forward to kiss her, his hands shifting beneath the top of her dress to push the material off her shoulders. When he moved away, her dress fell to her hips, and he stepped back to look at her. "You're beautiful," he said, tossing his shirt aside. He cupped her breasts and caressed her lightly with his thumbs. The sensations rocked her. Gasping, she closed her eyes and clung to him.

"Abby, I've dreamed of this moment," he whispered, straightening to frame her face with his hands. "I want you—you can't imagine how much," he said in a hoarse whisper.

Sliding her arms around his neck, she stood on tiptoe to kiss him. His arms banded her waist, crushing her to him as they kissed, hot passionate kisses that made her want to toss aside her caution. Kissing him was exciting beyond anything she had ever known or imagined.

She wanted him with her whole being while she felt it meant little to him, something casual that would not involve his heart. She didn't know whether she could deal with that.

She pulled away. "Josh, I didn't come to New York to sleep with you. It may happen, but I'm not ready at this point. I still feel we barely know each other. You said I had no obligations in accepting this trip."

"You don't," he said, caressing her throat, his breathing ragged as if he had run miles. "Absolutely not. I never want a woman in my arms out of a feeling of obligation." He pulled her dress back in place. "We'll slow down. We'll go sit on the balcony, sip our drinks and talk. How's that?" he asked. His voice was hoarse, and the hungry expression on his face made her want to step back into his embrace.

"For the moment, that may be a good idea," she replied in spite of what she felt.

He gazed at her a moment as if making a decision.

"Josh, this is amazing out here," she said. She stood at the rail of the balcony with her arms resting on it. Wind blew her long, wavy blond locks. Her back was bare, her legs shapely, and she looked beautiful. His mouth went dry. He had done what she wanted and what he should, but it had taken self-control. He wanted her in his arms and in his bed tonight, and he felt certain he could kiss away her objections, but he didn't want to go against her wishes.

"You don't have any vertigo, do you?" he asked.

"No, I love standing here and looking at the city, down below as well as far away. This is a fantastic view, and I'm enjoying it."

"I'm glad," he said, moving beside her and turning her to face him as he slipped an arm around her waist. "One kiss—just one, out here to remember this moment."

She didn't object, but stood looking at him with eyes open wide. He tightened his arm around her and leaned down to kiss her, opening her mouth with his, his tongue going over hers. She held him tightly, kissing him eagerly, making him almost regret his decision to limit himself to only one kiss.

He was aroused, wanting her, wishing he could unfasten her dress and toss it aside, take her to bed and make love to her.

Instead, at the first hint she was moving away, he released her. "Welcome to New York," he whispered.

"It's fabulous," she answered breathlessly.

"Want to sit?"

She moved to the chair by the table, and he sat beside her. "Josh, this hotel is so luxurious."

"I like it. This chain has done well, even though it's small next to two others I have. This is the deluxe line."

"This is like a dream."

"I'm glad. Part of this is a big thank you for taking me in out of that blizzard."

"It worked out, and you were so much help, I'm glad I did."

"Do you plan to always run the inn?"

"Probably so. Justin and Arden won't come back to run the place with me after they finish college, which is all right because I'm happy there. Justin is majoring in accounting and Arden is planning on law school. I expect them both to leave Beckett. They're on scholarships, and I help them with money from the inn, which is more profitable than Mom's hair shop."

"I think you told me that you didn't go to college."

"Right. I've always helped at the inn, and after high school I stepped in full-time, which I was happy to do. I've always planned to do that when I grew up. Pretty simple in your view, I'm sure. Your major was what?"

"Double major in accounting and agriculture. MBA in accounting. I played football and then pro ball until a shoulder injury sidelined me and I decided to move on. I invested my money in a small chain of hotels that I've been able to grow into a bigger chain, and I started the others. I've been fortunate to have inherited money, too."

"A very busy man."

"I've told you someday I'll be a rancher. I'd like you to see the ranch."

"I'd love that probably as much as this."

He smiled. "Right now, I thrive on business. I like my travels and making deals, the challenges and the satisfaction. But I do miss the ranch," he said with a wistful note in his voice.

"Josh, if you really love it, why are you staying in the business world when you can do what you really like best? I know you thrive in the corporate world, but you've said you love life on your ranch. You said I'm missing out on life. I still think you are, in a big way."

He ran his finger along her cheek. "You might be right," he said quietly. While they talked, he couldn't resist touching her. He held her hand, rubbing her knuckles lightly with his thumb. She had the softest skin, even though she worked with her hands constantly.

"Josh, the sun will come up in not too many hours. I should go to my suite."

"Sure," he said, draping his arm lightly across her shoulders. "I'll get the bottles—don't worry about them."

He walked her around to her door and waited while she unlocked it. He opened the door, held it for her and followed her inside, then caught her arm and turned her to face him. "I want a good-night kiss," he said, wanting even more to pick her up and carry her to bed. He wanted *her*. She was excited about their itinerary for tomorrow, but as far as he was concerned, they could chuck it and just make love all day.

Even more, he wanted her to be happy, so if it was seeing the sights that he had been to too many times to count since he was a kid, he would do that with her. She seemed dazzled by the city, while he was dazzled by her.

He poured his longing and passion into his kiss, which became kisses as he caressed her and ached to make love to her.

Finally she stopped him. "Josh, it really is late. You need to go."

He sighed. "Yeah, I know," he said in a gravelly voice. He ran his finger down her cheek. "Sometime I'm going to make love to you for hours," he whispered, determined that would happen before too long.

Wide-eyed and solemn, she gazed up at him. "It might happen, Josh. We both want that, even though that isn't the wisest course to follow. Once again, I had a wonderful time."

He barely heard her last words, because his heart pounded over her admission that she wanted the same lovemaking he did.

"I'm glad you had a good time. See you bright and early. We can do breakfast or bed," he said, teasing her.

She looked briefly startled and then laughed. "I believe I'll choose breakfast. You remember that."

"How could I forget?" He brushed her lips lightly with another kiss and left.

After saying good-night to Josh, Abby drifted through the suite and opened her balcony door to peep outside, seeing Josh wasn't out. She sat on the balcony, loving every minute of her stay at his hotel. He hadn't wanted to stop making love tonight and neither had she, but she didn't want to go home with big regrets. She wanted to be sure of what she did.

Finally, when she was about to fall asleep, she went inside, closing up and getting ready for bed. She left a wake-up call and fell asleep almost as soon as she stretched out in bed.

Josh had the entire day planned, and an early stop was the Empire State Building. She stood looking at the view. "It's a gorgeous morning, I'm at the Empire State Building and we have to take a selfie to send home."

"First let me take some pictures of you to send home. They'll want to see you," he said, snapping pictures with her phone. Impulsively, he pulled out his own phone and took her picture as she laughed.

She took a selfie of the two of them and looked at it. She had on black slacks and a black cotton shirt with a matching sweater on over it. Josh was dressed in his brown sweater, brown slacks and boots. Josh reached out to get her phone. "I'll take the next selfie of us," he said, wrapping his arms around her, snapping a picture while they kissed.

"I'm not sending that one home."

"You don't want to be seen kissing me?"

She smiled. "I'll answer that later today."

He grinned and took her arm. "On to the next tour stop."

They went to St. Patrick's Cathedral, saw Grand Central Terminal and walked up Fifth Avenue into Central Park. "Josh, this park is marvelous. I've seen it in movies, but real life is better."

As the day wore on, she took pictures of bridges she had also seen in movies while Josh patiently waited and then took her to the next thing to see.

It was late in the afternoon when they went to the Statue of Liberty. In the midst of the crowd, she took out her phone, wrapped her arm around his neck to kiss him and took a picture of them. The moment she kissed him, his arms circled her waist and he held her tightly, kissing her in return, making far more of the kiss than she had ever intended. When he released her, she had a moment when she was still lost in his kiss, forgetting everything around them.

"I told you I would give you an answer later. No, I don't mind being seen kissing you," she said, but he had turned the kiss into a fiery moment that ignited passion.

He smiled. "It's a good thing, because it'll probably happen again while we're out. Your enthusiasm and exuberance about everything makes you irresistible. Plus there are a few other reasons you're irresistible."

"No one has ever told me that before. We won't go into the other reasons. At least not out in public. You're a bit irresistible yourself. Maybe someday I'll tell you why."

"That's something I'd like to hear. C'mon, time to get the ferry back."

They returned to the hotel to change for dinner. She showered and dried her hair, trying to get her unruly curls under control, momentarily envious of Josh's short brown hair.

She slipped into the other dress she had bought. It was wine-colored with long sleeves, clinging, longer than the black dress, with a slit on one side of the skirt. The cowl neck was low-cut. She wore the black high-heeled sandals with it.

She pinned her hair back slightly on either side of her head, working to brush out the curls and leave it in soft waves falling freely a few inches over her shoulders as her stylist at the salon had done yesterday.

Picking up her phone, she looked at pictures from their day. She had had the most wonderful time possible with Josh, but that didn't change one bit of the huge differences in their lives, lifestyles, ambitions and future plans. He would never fall in love with her, and she had to keep that in mind, because she was already in love with him. She hated to view her feelings too closely this weekend when she was with him. She was having the time of her life, an unforgettable time, she was sure. Would heartbreak go with it?

She still hadn't made a decision whether they would make love or not. All her decisions about no sex before marriage had been made long ago without Josh in the equation, and she didn't want him to change them now.

She heard a knock and went to the door, opening it to face him. He made her heart thud. He was in a navy suit with a matching navy tie. Gold cuff links in his dress shirt French cuffs added a touch of elegance to his appearance.

"I have to say wow," he told her. "You look stunning."

"Thank you, thank you," she said, smiling at him. "And so do you."

"That's good to hear. Ready?"

"Oh, yes. You know I can't wait." She picked up her purse and jacket and closed her suite door.

He took her arm. "Tonight we're going to my favorite restaurant. American, steak and potatoes, but they have other choices. How's that?"

"As wonderful as French. I'll love it if you do."

"You're being happy and cooperative."

"Always," she said, laughing, and he smiled at her.

"We have this elevator all to ourselves," he said, holding her arm lightly and leaning close to kiss her.

Her heart missed a beat the minute his mouth touched hers. Even a light, quick elevator kiss set her pulse racing when it was Josh.

This restaurant, too, was high in a building with a spectacular view that she couldn't stop looking at as they walked through the carpeted, dimly lit dining room. A piano player provided soft music, and their table offered a view of the glittering city. A candle was on the white linen-covered table, and someone was there to wait on them almost instantly.

They both ordered steaks and Josh ordered wine. "I did see couples on the dance floor. Care to dance?"

"I'd love to," she said, taking his offered hand. She stepped into his arms, dancing with him, knowing she would remember this weekend the rest of her life.

They spent more time dancing than eating. Of all the men for her to enjoy being with, why was it a mogul whose life was so far removed from her own?

As she laughed at something he told her, she gazed into his dark eyes and knew she would never have more fun than she had had with him. She didn't think she could possibly ever have kisses as hot and passionate, either. And she didn't think she would ever go back to dating Lamont or ever marry him. After seeing New York, she realized there was way too much in life to go back to playing it safe and accepting the most convenient way of living. She had accused Josh of missing out on life, but she saw now that he wasn't the only one. She could get out and live a fuller life.

At midnight, as they finished a dance, Josh took her hand to walk back to their table. "Ready to go to the hotel? We'll talk, kiss and look at the view—or do you want to stay here longer?"

"Let's go back to the hotel."

"Good. That's what I'd hoped you would say."

At the hotel, when they walked toward the balcony with their drinks, he set their glasses on a table, her heart beating faster as she anticipated his kiss.

He drew her to him. "Before we go out on the balcony, which is relatively private, but not private enough, come here."

Her heart thudded as she walked into his embrace and raised her face for his kiss. Desire filled his dark eyes when he looked at her, and then his gaze shifted to her mouth. He leaned down to kiss her.

He held her tightly, bending over her so she had to

cling to him as she kissed him in return. She moaned softly with pleasure from his kisses that were endless, seemingly more passionate each time. She felt his fingers at her back and then felt the cool air as Josh drew the zipper of her dress slowly down her back, opening her dress to push it off. It fell with a soft whoosh around her ankles, and she stepped out of it and her high heels.

With trembling fingers, she unfastened his shirt and pushed it away, running her hands over his muscled chest while his kisses drove all thoughts from her mind. She just wanted to keep kissing him. She wanted the clothing barriers away. This whole weekend had been a once-in-a-lifetime experience, and she wasn't going to stop now. Josh would never fall in love with her. She would go home, get over this trip, settle back into her regular life and someday marry, living in Beckett for the rest of her life.

This one night was the exception to all of the life she had planned for so long. She wanted Josh's kisses, his loving, all of him. She didn't want to look back with regrets of what she'd missed or had denied herself. She unfastened his belt, then his trousers to push them off, and he stepped out of them. He was aroused, ready to love. She wanted his arms around her and his kisses. He peeled away her lace panties. Her bra was gone swiftly.

He cupped her breasts in his hands, caressing her as he ran his thumbs so lightly over her. "You're beautiful, every inch of you," he said in a voice hoarse with passion. As she touched him, his deep, sexy kisses made her tremble.

She ran her hands over his chest, up to touch his jaw, feeling slight stubble. Trailing her fingers over the angular planes of his face, she wanted to commit everything to memory that happened this night. His chest was hard with sculpted muscles, his biceps well-defined.

Could she let go of the restrictions she had always held to? This was the one chance in her life to make love wildly, passionately and in a manner she didn't expect to again.

He picked her up to carry her near the bed, switching on a small table lamp and yanking covers back before turning to look at her again. "Abby, you're gorgeous," he said in the same gruff voice.

Standing her on her feet, he embraced and kissed her. His erection pressed against her, hot, hard. She moved her hand down his smooth back over firm buttocks and down to muscled thighs.

He stepped back to look at her again, filling each hand with a breast and leaning down to kiss her, his tongue sending streaks of pleasure that made her gasp, close her eyes and cling to his shoulders. "Josh," she whispered, feeling on fire, wanting to spread her legs for him, wanting him to love her for hours.

He kissed first one breast and then the other, caressing her at the same time. She gasped as sensations rocked her. She wanted to press her hips against him, but he held her away as he fondled and kissed her breasts.

She was barely aware when Josh picked her up to place her on the bed. Kneeling beside her, he stroked her ankle, moving up her leg, his fingers stroking lightly, his tongue and lips following as he caressed behind her knee. He moved between her legs, his hands stroking her inner thighs, driving her wild with desire.

He leaned down to kiss her thighs, his tongue following where his hands had been.

"Josh," she gasped and sat up to hold him and kiss him, running her tongue over him. His rod was hot, thick and hard. As she stroked him, he wound his fingers in her hair. He groaned and kissed her passionately until they fell back on the bed, and he showered her with kisses while he caressed her.

"Wait," he said and stepped off the bed. He returned to move between her legs and put on a condom.

Breathlessly she gazed at him. He was handsome, thrilling, sexy. She wanted him, reaching out to rest her hands on his thighs, feeling the crisp short hairs beneath her palms.

He lowered himself, his dark eyes watching her as he kissed her. She closed her eyes, wrapping her arms around him.

He started to enter her, moving slowly, and then he stopped.

"Abby, are you sure you want this? You're a virgin," he said, frowning.

She locked her legs around him and held him more tightly to pull him to her. "Love me now. I know what I want." She ran her hands down his back and over his buttocks. "Josh, I want you."

He lowered himself again and thrust into her. She felt a sharp pain as he covered her mouth with his to kiss her, and then she moved with him. Pain and pleasure mixed and then urgency made her move wildly beneath him, rocking with him and finally having a burst of release with her climax while he shuddered with his at the same time.

They gradually slowed, and his breathing became normal when he turned to kiss her lightly.

"Abby, you're special," he whispered.

Wrapped in euphoria, she drew him to her to kiss him again. Holding her, he rolled on his side, keeping her close with him and their legs entwined.

She held him tightly, at the moment enveloped in bliss. Josh was hers right now, and tomorrow didn't exist. For tonight she would take the moments, cherish Josh, making love with him. This was perfection, what she had dreamed of, wanted, fantasized about, this never-to-be-forgotten night and weekend. She suspected no one would ever excite her as much as he did.

She was in love with him—or had she been in love with him before this weekend ever started? She didn't want him to know. When he walked away—and she was certain he would—she didn't want him to feel guilty. She wanted him to think her heart was no more involved than his was.

She stroked his back, feeling the solid muscles, his narrow waist. She was eager to hold and touch him the rest of the night.

"I'm glad you came to New York," he said in his husky voice. "A rare night, a unique woman in my arms." He kissed her lightly again.

"It's thrilling, and I'll always remember this weekend."

"Both of us will," he whispered.

He held her quietly for some time and finally shifted to look at her. "How about a hot tub?"

"I'm not sure I can move," she said.

"I'll carry you." Stepping out of bed, he picked her up. She wrapped her arms around his neck and kissed him as he walked toward the bathroom. Shortly they were in a tub of hot water. She sat back between his legs, leaning against him while they talked, going from topic to topic. She felt deeply relaxed, floating in euphoria, happy with him, with everything about the evening.

When they finally climbed out of the tub, they dried each other with slow, sensual strokes, Josh barely touching her with the towel as he drew it across her breasts while his dark gaze conveyed so much desire, she could barely get her breath.

Inhaling deeply, she reached for him. He stepped close to wrap his arms around her and kissed her passionately, a searing, possessive kiss as if she was the only woman ever to be in his life. How could he make her feel so special, so pretty in his eyes?

She responded to him, pouring her heart into her kisses, sliding her hands over him, caressing him, hoping to drive him to the trembling need she felt.

As he kissed her, his hands were all over her, touching her lightly, moving between her legs to touch and rub her intimately, building her need.

He carried her to bed to kiss and caress her, taking his time until she tugged at his shoulders. "Josh, I want you now," she whispered, looking up at him and then pulling him down to kiss him hungrily. He reached to the table by the bed to get protection.

Lowering himself, he entered her, moving slowly, letting desire and need build. She clung to him, aware only of Josh, his muscled body, his hands and mouth, his staff, thick, hot and hard, driving her to moving wildly beneath him until she reached a pounding climax.

She shook with release, sending Josh into his climax, as he held her tightly and they moved together. She heard his groan, felt his arms tighten around her. Her breathing was ragged, loud as she gasped for each breath and slowed, sinking into rapture that was even greater than the first time with him.

How could she not fall more deeply in love with him after this night? She wouldn't think about the answer. Instead, she kissed him and held him tightly. For tonight there were no problems, and that was enough for the moment.

* * *

When sunlight spilled through the windows in the morning, Josh held her close against him. He turned on his side to prop himself up to look at her. Short locks of brown hair fell over his forehead, and she combed them back gently with her fingers. Everything about him fascinated her, and she couldn't stop touching him. She ran her hand over his shoulder. "I can tell you work out."

"Yes. I'll return to ranch life someday, and I don't want to be too puny to do it."

She smiled. "I don't think you're in danger of being too puny. Definitely not too puny to make love."

He smiled. "We go home this afternoon. I thought I would take you out for breakfast, but would you like to have breakfast on our balcony? I'll call room service."

"I would love breakfast on our balcony if it isn't cold out there."

"If it is, we'll have breakfast in here. I'll get the menu, and you can tell me what you want."

He stepped out of bed and grabbed a towel he had dropped the night before to wrap around him, knotting it across his flat stomach.

She propped up pillows, sat up and pulled a sheet under her arms to cover her. He came back and handed her the menu as he slid beneath the covers and tossed away the towel.

"Now what do you see that you'd like?"

"What I see is a very handsome man, and I'd like him to kiss me," she said, studying him. His expression changed, and he turned to take her into his arms. He pulled her onto his lap as he wrapped his arms around her to kiss her.

Over an hour later, Josh asked her again what she'd like for breakfast. "That question worked out well last time, so I'll try it again," he said.

Smiling, she leaned over the edge of the bed to pull up the menu and look at it. "This time I'll order, because I'm definitely getting hungry."

In half an hour, they sat in plush bathrobes on the balcony while they ate.

"Josh, I love this view," she said, pulling her cell phone from her robe pocket. She turned to face him. "Can I take your picture?"

"In this robe?"

"Yes. Is that okay?"

"Sure, if this is what you want."

She took his picture, smiling at him. "Every minute has been special."

"I can say the same, Abby," he told her, suddenly looking at her with an earnest expression that faded into another smile as he reached for her. "Come home with me to the ranch. We can leave this afternoon and get in tonight. Stay a couple of nights, and then I'll take you home."

She stared at him while she debated what to do. He leaned close to caress her nape lightly. "Your family can work it out, and it's just this once. I want to show you my ranch."

She nodded. "If someone will cover for me, I will. I'll call now."

Taking her phone, she walked away from him to talk to her mother briefly about going with him to his ranch. She talked quietly, ending with thanks.

"Mom said the desk at the inn will be covered and to have a good time," she said, not mentioning that her mother had said, "Take real good care of yourself" before she ended the call. She was certain her mother worried about her having a broken heart over Josh. "I need to go home Tuesday," she said breathlessly, and his eyes narrowed slightly. "I've finished my breakfast."

He stood and came around to pick her up and carry her to the bedroom. Dropping the robe, she slid beneath the sheet with him and slipped her arm around his neck while her other hand moved beneath the sheet to fondle him. He was aroused, ready to love again. He lifted her over him, so she sat astride him.

She wrapped her arms around his neck and leaned in a few inches to look at him. "I can't get enough of you," she whispered.

"I hope you can't," he answered as he reached out to cup her breasts and shower kisses over first one and then the other. He moved her closer, entering her with urgency as if it were the first time they had loved.

Later they sat on the balcony again after ordering a light lunch. "Josh, this is wonderful," she said.

"You like the whole world. Have you ever been any-place you didn't like?" he asked, sounding amused, and she stopped viewing the skyline to turn to him.

"No, I suppose I haven't. I don't travel much, so when I do, I like the places I've gone. Some are more spectacular than others, and this is definitely the most spectacular of all and the best—as Arden would say, 'awesome.' It really is awesome. The description fits this city."

"I'll have to say, you've taken to it better than I thought you might. Maybe better than I ever have," he added, glancing out at the skyline. "When I think of New York City, I think of sirens through the night, crowds of people, trying to get a cab in a storm, although I usually have a limo now—"

"For a man who's so much fun to be with, that's a harsh outlook."

"I've been coming here off and on since I was about ten years old. My family came a lot when I was a kid and later, I have to come on business. Sometimes I get jaded about things and places that I've seen a lot."

"Well, keep your sunny side up while you're with me, please. I like that."

"If it pleases you, then I will do my best to do what you want."

She smiled at him. "Why do I have such fun with you? You're a charmer. I can answer my own question."

"And that's a negative in your view."

"It has a definite appeal. You know you make my heart go pitter-pat."

"I hope so, and in a minute we're going to forget about the food that's—" They heard knocking.

"There he is," Josh said, standing. "I'll take care of it." He left, and she turned back to look out over buildings. Some were taller than the hotel. She could see the rooftops of others, with penthouses, or gardens and trees growing in large planters, a life so different from her own that she still felt dazzled by the city. And dazzled by Josh, more in love with him each hour. She was certain his feelings for her were shallow and nothing like what she felt for him.

She hoped she could return to her plain way of life in Beckett easily and tuck this time with Josh away in her memories as once-in-a-lifetime fun, sexy and amazing. She knew her relationship with Lamont was over. She could never go back to that, and it wasn't fair for Lamont, either. They weren't in love or deeply attracted. It had just been convenient.

Her thoughts shifted to Josh. Even if he fell wildly

in love—which she was sensible enough to know he would not—she couldn't tie her life to a charmer, a worldly man who could sweet-talk her into doing what he wanted and then, like her father, just disappear out of her life someday. Or even if he didn't disappear, just want out of any relationship with her.

She expected them never to get to the relationship stage, though. She didn't want to risk that much. If she got into a relationship with Josh and then he ended it, she would be brokenhearted to the point that she could never get over it. She wasn't certain her mother had ever gotten over her father or stopped loving him.

Interrupting her thoughts, a waiter pushed a cart onto the balcony and began transferring covered dishes to the table in front of them, sandwiches, bowls of chips, various fruits and desserts.

As they ate, she was still lost in thought. Was this weekend something she would recall with joy, or would it always remind her of how plain her life was in Beckett? Was the handsome charmer sitting so close to her going to break her heart? Had she already set herself up for a lasting hurt?

Eight

They scrapped the sightseeing plans to start home to Josh's ranch at one that afternoon, arriving in Dallas and changing planes to fly to Verity, where Josh had a car waiting. Leaving Verity at dusk, he drove across mesquite-covered land much like land around Beckett.

When they left the county road to drive over the bumpy pipes of the cattle guard, they passed beneath a high black iron arch with a circle centered at the top. Inside the circle was JC Ranch in iron, showing clearly in the bright glow from a spotlight.

After he had driven ten minutes without a sign of life, she was surprised. "How far away is your house?"

"Pretty dang far," he answered. "I don't want to be living near the county road where I see traffic if I look out my windows or where people driving past can see my house and all the other structures. I want to be back where I see open land and country, not a highway."

"No danger of that," she replied, unable to imagine Josh living in isolation. Darkness enveloped them except for the sweep of his headlights until they topped a small hill. Far ahead she saw myriad lights.

In a short time, they began to pass lighted barns, corrals and outbuildings. Most of her attention went to a sprawling gray slate stacked stone ranch house with a wraparound porch, wood railings, two porch swings and old-fashioned rocking chairs. Lights illuminated massive live oaks that had to be older than Josh. In front of the house was a pond with lighted fountains.

"I don't know why you ever leave this." She viewed it as beautiful, peaceful and welcoming.

"I'm beginning to wonder myself," he said, sounding unusually solemn. "Have you ever ridden a horse?"

"Sure. You don't grow up in Beckett without knowing someone with horses."

"Want to ride early in the morning? I have a gentle horse for you."

"I'd like that," she said.

"Later we'll go out in the truck, and I'll show you more of the ranch. Tomorrow night, how about barbeque and a little dancing—two-stepping?"

"It all sounds fun," she answered. "Remember, I have to get home Tuesday. Mom has customers booked at her hair shop, and my sis and brother have school."

"I'll get you home early Tuesday, I promise."

Soon he drove on a circular drive to a back door and stepped out. A man got up from one of the rocking chairs and came toward them. "Howdy, Josh. Let me get your things."

"Told you that you didn't need to wait for us to come in," Josh said, taking her arm. "Abby, meet Hitch Watkinson, my foreman. Hitch, this is Abby Donovan from Beckett, Texas."

"Glad to meet you, Miss Donovan," Hitch said.

"I'm glad to meet you," she replied, smiling at the tall, black-haired man with a deeply tanned face and a black broad-brimmed hat on his head.

"Just set everything in the hall, Hitch. I'll take it from there."

"Sure. Glad to have you home."

Josh unlocked a door and opened it. "We'll have the house to ourselves until morning, and then my staff will appear."

Hitch brought their things inside, said goodbye and left.

She stood in a long hall with Western paintings on the walls, walnut furniture and potted plants. Various hallways branched off to different wings of the house. "I'll show you around."

"Did you leave all the lights on when you left?"

"No. Hitch has a key. He came in and turned lights on for us when I texted him that we were coming. There is also a very full fridge should we want anything to eat.

"This is a huge house," she said. "It seems far bigger than the inn. How many bedrooms?"

"Seven," he said. "Actually five suites plus two more bedrooms. Sometimes I have all the family here. I have company during hunting season. There are four guesthouses on the ranch. Some people who work here have homes on the property, too. Hitch for one. Let's take our things upstairs first, and then I'll give you a tour."

He shouldered bags, and she took one. They climbed a sweeping spiral staircase to the second floor and walked down another large hallway.

"Here's my bedroom," he said, leading her into a sitting room larger than the main living room at her inn. The furniture was Western with brown leather wingback chairs and a long brown leather sofa that faced a massive stone fireplace. Bookshelves lined one wall while another wall was glass. In the light that spilled in from outside, she could see a broad covered balcony with black wrought iron furniture. He tossed bags onto a chair and closed the drapes before turning to walk back to her and take her bag to place it on another chair.

"Josh this is a beautiful home," she said, thinking about him sleeping on her short sofa for three nights.

She wondered again why Josh had asked her to go with him to New York. She couldn't imagine the man who lived in this palatial home wanting to spend a weekend with her. She suspected he'd dated models, maybe actresses, women who were breathtakingly beautiful and had lives far more interesting that running a bed-and-breakfast in a small west Texas town.

"I'm glad we didn't come here first. I think I would have backed out of the trip. I can't imagine why you would want to take someone like me to New York."

He slipped his arms around her waist and gazed into her eyes. "I asked you to go with me because I wanted to be with you more than anyone else. Anyone," he repeated with emphasis. "I've had a grand time, and I don't want the weekend to end. That's why I asked you here tonight. You're the first woman I've ever brought to stay in this house."

Startled, she stared at him while her heart pounded. If only he really cared. But she knew better, no matter what he said now. There was no way, and even if he did, he wasn't the man for her. He was the man she had vowed all her adult life that she would avoid falling in love with. She was already in love with him, but she didn't want to go any farther. This was not the man to settle and lead a quiet life with a woman like her. Not ever. She hadn't changed her feelings about men like her father.

"Josh, this has been a wonderful weekend. I don't expect any more than that, and you and I are definitely not right for each other."

He tightened his arms around her, his eyes darkening with passion. He leaned down to kiss her, his mouth covering hers. It was a demanding, possessive kiss that made her feel as if he was in love, as if she was the one woman he wanted, yet she still clung to the knowledge that she was fooling herself and he would never really feel that way.

And then she stopped thinking and tossed caution and wisdom aside, holding him and kissing him in return, spiraling into passion and forgetting the world and all problems.

She was barely aware when he picked her up to carry her to his big bed.

It was in the early hours of the morning when Josh stirred and shifted, looking at Abby in the crook of his arm, lying against him, warm and soft. He brushed a silky lock of her hair away from her face. He couldn't understand his own reactions to her. He couldn't get enough of her.

He thought this weekend would satisfy him and he would lose interest. He had lost interest fast in some women he had dated, but it hadn't worked that way with Abby. Why was she such a draw to him when she was so many things he didn't like? She had been a virgin, which had shocked him and still made him wonder how

important their lovemaking was to her since he was the
first and only man she had ever been intimate with.

Her reactions weren't what he would have guessed.
When she let him seduce her, take her virginity, he
thought she might expect a relationship with him. That
hadn't happened. She still viewed him as an undesir-
able male for a long-term relationship. If he hadn't been
so tied up in knots with wanting her, he would have
laughed at himself and his ego for assuming she would
be dazzled by the first man she had sex with. Along
with being a caring person, she was a confident woman
and knew what she wanted in life. He suspected she
would stick to her principles and views of what she
wanted and didn't want. Why was he so upset that he
fell into the "didn't want" category? He shouldn't care
and he should be relieved, but he did care and he wasn't
relieved at all.

They shouldn't be compatible. Was it purely sex?
Since there hadn't been any sex until Saturday night and
he had spent time with her at the inn and Friday night
in New York, he didn't see how it could be purely lust.

He hadn't thought beyond this weekend. His plan
was a fun weekend in New York, then take her home
and forget her. That was what she wanted him to do.
She wasn't thrilled with him at all. He wasn't the type of
man she wanted in her life. It was Lamont she wanted.
How could he be so drawn to a woman who was drawn
to a man like Lamont?

Josh looked at her smooth, flawless skin, her long
lashes, her silky hair that fell in waves over her bare
shoulders and the pillow. He shook his head. He couldn't
figure out his own feelings. Right now he wanted to
wake her and make love. It had to be pure lust because
they had nothing else between them. But if there was

nothing between them, why had he wanted to take her to his ranch?

He thought about making arrangements to see her again. Beckett, Texas, was not convenient for a relationship. He mulled over possibilities. He hadn't thought she would go to New York with him when he asked her, but she had. Perhaps she'd go on other adventures with him. He needed to get over wanting to be with her. She wasn't his type. He wasn't her type. Once he was back in his regular routine, he would forget her.

He lay on his back and stared into the room. A small lamp burned, and he reached over to switch it off. Darkness enveloped them, but he didn't think he would sleep much. He turned, taking her into his arms and holding her close.

She sighed, tightened her arms around him and held him. Her breathing was deep and even, so she still slept. He wanted to kiss her awake and make love, but he let her sleep while he tried to figure why he wanted so badly to be with her.

Monday morning had spun away into afternoon when they got out of bed for Josh to cook breakfast. She took over and he helped.

"Our horseback ride will have to be another day. Which means you'll have to come back again," he said, smiling at her with a flash of white teeth. He reached across the table to take her hand. "I'd like you to come back, Abby," he said.

"Thank you," she said, knowing she never would be back. She withdrew her hand to eat her breakfast. "When did you buy this ranch?"

"As soon as I could when I graduated from college," he said, telling her about the ranch as they ate toast and scrambled eggs. There were bowls of strawberries, blueberries and blackberries with slices of kiwi. China cups held steaming coffee, and tall glasses were chilled with orange juice.

"Maybe breakfast is lunch, too," she said. "It's late enough to be lunch."

"After we eat, we can drive around the ranch. Or we can just go back to my bedroom."

She paused and shook her head. "I'm going to opt to see the ranch because this will be my only chance."

"On this trip," he said.

It was an hour later when she met him in the hall, ready to see the property.

Looking very much the rancher, he wore a blue denim shirt and jeans, a broad-brimmed brown hat, a hand-tooled belt and his boots.

"You look great," he said, his gaze sweeping over her. She thought she didn't look any different in her pink sweater, jeans and suede boots from when he saw her at the inn except for her hair, which she still let fall freely.

It was a crisp spring afternoon with blue skies and a stiff breeze. As they headed out, Josh pulled on a denim jacket and gave her one of his to wear. In the truck, he talked about cattle and horses, and she could tell that he enjoyed the ranch and knew a lot about it for someone who was rarely there.

Josh pulled over to show her an ancient windmill that he had left standing because it was so old. They drove past a small sod house that was even older than the windmill and on the ranch when he bought it. Later he drove to a spot with three tall cottonwoods. They climbed out of the truck to walk to a creek that widened into a small pool before narrowing to a creek again. Jake sat on a boulder and helped her sit down beside him, keeping his arm around her.

"This is one of my favorite places. In the summer, it's cool here, shady and quiet except for the water spilling over those rocks and into the pool. Some former owner hauled these rocks in here to create this pool, and it's pleasant. Sometimes I come sit for a while, just sit and be quiet. It's a good place to think and just do nothing except enjoy the ranch."

"Maybe you're not missing out on life as much as I thought," she said, surprised he experienced such moments as he had just described.

"I have to admit, I haven't been in this spot for two or three years. Those times are coming more seldom now because I'm so damn busy."

"Maybe you should try to work the ranch into your schedule more often."

"I've been thinking about it more and more. Actually, you make me think about it more," he said.

"How so?" she asked.

"I guess all your talk about enjoying life. This is the life I really like."

"Yet you choose to live in the corporate world. I'm returning to my opinion that you're missing out on life."

He gave her a crooked smile. "After the way you've taken to New York and come here with me and a few other things, I have to take back my judgment that *you're* missing out on life. I suppose you're not so much because you wring the most satisfaction out of every minute. You're easy to please, which makes a difference."

As they lapsed into silence, she listened to water spilling out of the pool, meandering on downstream, and thought about Josh's life.

Finally he stood and offered his hand. "We'll head back and get ready for tonight." She couldn't help but notice that he seemed lost in thought.

It was almost eight that evening when they entered the noisy, crowded honky-tonk. Fiddlers and a guitar player with a keyboard accompaniment provided the music. As soon as they had ordered a beer and a lemonade, he took her hand to dance.

They scooted around the floor with other couples, Abby watching Josh and desire building. Tonight, with his white Stetson, a navy Western-style shirt, a wide hand-tooled belt, tight jeans and boots, he was the most handsome man in the place or whom she had ever known, for that matter, and he looked every inch the wealthy rancher.

He seemed to know more than half the people present, speaking briefly to folks when they'd walked in and all the way to their table, then, speaking to more as they'd walked to the dance floor.

She already anticipated leaving. This was their last night together, and she wanted his kisses more than ever, wanted to be in his arms and make love again. He had changed her life. Tomorrow held uncertainties and questions, yet she wouldn't go back and undo meeting Josh and all that had happened since for anything.

They danced three dances and the set ended. As they stood talking, waiting for the musicians to start again, a tall, brown-haired cowboy approached them.

"Howdy, Mr. Calhoun."

"Evening, Johnny Frank."

"Haven't seen you here in a long time."

"Nope. I haven't been home in a long time. This is Abby Donovan. Abby, meet Johnny Frank Smith."

"You're not from around here, are you?" Johnny Frank asked her.

"No, I'm from Beckett, Texas."

"Mr. Calhoun, would you mind if I dance with Miss Donovan?" Johnny Frank asked.

"That's up to her," Josh said.

Johnny Frank turned to smile at Abby, and she smiled in return. "Thank you. That's nice. Since I came with Josh, I better stay with Josh, but I do thank you for asking, and I'm glad to have met you."

"Sure, ma'am. Thanks. See you both," he said, grinning and walking away.

"Thank you for turning him down," Josh said. "I see other guys watching, and I think we may have an evening of invitations for you, although since you discouraged Johnny Frank, we might not. But I'm ready to toss in the towel and go back to the ranch, where I can have you all to myself. Would you mind?"

She laughed. "I don't mind. I'd prefer that, too."

"You don't have to tell me twice," he said, slipping his arm around her waist possessively and heading for the door.

Outside she laughed. "That was mighty short, but fun."

"Well, I think if we'd stayed, you could have been the belle of the ball. You watch. Johnny Frank will come to Beckett and look you up."

"I doubt that," she said.

His arm tightened around her waist as he halted and turned her to face him, wrapping both arms around her and leaning down to kiss her hard, possessively. Everything else ceased to exist except Josh as she clung to him and kissed him in return.

Finally, when he released her, both of them were

breathing hard. "Let's get home where we'll be alone," he said, holding her close as they hurried to his pickup.

As they sped back to the ranch along the dark county road, she watched him drive. Light from the dash reflected on his face, highlighting his prominent cheekbones, throwing his cheeks into shadow. He had not shaved and had a slight growth of dark stubble that fit with their entertainment for the evening and made him look more like one of the cowboys.

"You're very quiet," she said.

"Thanks again for turning Johnny Frank down. I wanted to punch him out."

"Good heavens. I'm glad you restrained yourself."

"I wouldn't have hit him. I've never done anything like that except to defend myself, but I still didn't want you to dance with him. You bring out reactions in me I've never had before, and I'm having experiences with you I've never had before."

"I can certainly say the same thing about you," she said, not about to tell him that he had changed her life. "The only new experiences I can think you've had are sleeping on my short sofa and maybe asking Mr. Hickman to go fishing. Perhaps washing dishes and shoveling my drive and all that work you did."

"Nope. I've done plenty of that kind of work as a kid. And I've slept in worse places. I was so thankful to have that short sofa—you'll never know how glad I was to find a place to stay."

She lapsed into quiet, gazing out the window at the dark landscape and a myriad of twinkling stars overhead while she thought about her weekend with him.

When they walked into his house, he turned to draw her close again. "I can't get enough of you," he whispered before his mouth covered hers and prevented an answer.

* * *

The next day, he took her to the plane that would fly her back to Beckett. He stood at the foot of the steps and faced her, unable to resist touching her. He rested his hands lightly on her slender shoulders. It surprised him how much he wanted her to stay longer. He touched a long lock of her silky hair and then pulled her woolen jacket closer under her chin, little touches he wasn't sure why he needed. All he knew was he didn't want to tell her goodbye. "The weekend was great and it was special," he said.

"It was for me, too, Josh. Thank you for everything."

"When you land in Beckett, Benny will meet you and take you to the inn." Josh pulled her to him to kiss her. When he released her, he gazed at her. "I don't want to let you go."

Her blue eyes darkened slightly. "I think you have to," she said.

"I really don't want to. Abby, travel with me. I can hire someone to run the inn for you," he said, his words spilling out fast. "Come travel with me and live with me. It'll be like the weekend only even better, and I can show you the world."

Her eyes widened until he felt as if he would be consumed by a look. "We would have a wonderful time together."

"Josh, I can't do that. I have family and responsibilities."

"I'd cover the responsibilities for you. You can see your family whenever you want. I can easily afford to hire people to run the bed-and-breakfast whenever you're not there."

"I can't live with you. I just can't. My answer is a definite no, and I don't even have to think about it."

"I want you to think about it."

She shook her head. "No, it would never work, and I wouldn't be happy. Don't make this weekend a mistake. It's been wonderful, like a dream. Let's keep it that way, but you and I don't have a future. I really don't have one that would include moving in and traveling with you," she said. The tone of her voice became frosty. "That's not my life and never will be."

Her words were firm, and he stepped back. "I'll be in touch. You take care," he said.

"Thank you." She turned to hurry up the steps into the plane and reappeared at a window. She waved and he returned the wave. He turned around to walk away because the plane would take off soon.

The invitation to move in with him and travel with him had been impulsive, not even like him, because he usually thought things through. But it hadn't mattered because she wouldn't accept his offer. Not only that, but he also had a feeling she was insulted that he would even ask. He hadn't meant to offend her—far from it. He wanted her with him and he wanted to see her again. He didn't want goodbye.

He took a deep breath. He needed to forget her and go on with his life because they had no future together. He suspected she would not go away for another weekend with him.

As he climbed into his vehicle the white Calhoun plane took off in the distance. He paused, certain she was flying out of his life.

In Beckett, Benny met her and took her things to place them in his cab. As they headed toward town and the inn, he glanced at her in the rearview mirror. "I heard you've been to New York. What was it like?"

She smiled, glancing at him in the mirror as he returned his attention to the road. "It's a wonderful city with so much to do. If I lived there, I don't think I could ever do all I want."

"So you had a good time. You were with Josh Calhoun. He's really a nice guy."

"Yes, he is, Benny. He helped me a lot at the inn while Justin and Arden were gone."

"That's him. He tipped me the biggest tip I've ever had or ever will have. I think that's mostly because I tried so hard to find him a place to stay."

"That was very nice of you, and he told me. He really appreciated your help."

"He made that obvious. What did you see in New York?"

While she told him, she thought about Josh and being with him for the weekend. It had been wonderful, a dream come true until time to board the plane, when he asked her to move in with him and travel with him. In that moment, he was clearly the man she had expected him to be all the time. The charmer who was not into lasting relationships. His invitation had been a big reminder that she needed to put some space between herself and Josh, which shouldn't be difficult to do because time and distance would separate them anyway. She tried to pay attention to Benny's questions about New York and knew she would have another barrage of questions at the inn.

To her relief, when she arrived, Justin was in charge. He would ask her fewer questions than her mom would have and go on with talking about his own life.

She went to her room to change and put away her things. When she entered her sitting room, she thought of Josh there, remembered kissing him in this room, memories now that hurt.

Her cell phone rang, and she saw it was call from him. She didn't feel like taking it, so she dropped the phone back into her pocket.

She changed, heard the phone again and saw it was Josh once more. She let it ring. She wasn't ready to talk yet. She felt on a rocky emotional edge. She would have to get Josh out of her life, and it was going to hurt to do so. It already hurt to have him ask her to travel with him and live with him, to have him ask her to toss her life and family aside for his pleasure. She was sure he would compensate her with dresses and other gifts that really weren't that important to her. At the moment, she didn't want either of the dresses he had bought for her. If only he had just ended their amazing weekend without asking her to travel with him. She was determined to get him out of her thoughts and out of her life. There was no way to ever get him out of her memories.

Carrying souvenirs for Justin and Arden, she left her suite. As she walked down the hall, the elevator doors opened and Lamont emerged with briefcase in hand.

"Lamont, hello," she said, smiling, feeling a sense of dread, which she hoped she hid.

He paused. "Abby. So you're back. How was New York?"

"I did a lot of tourist things and had fun. Are you here to see Mr. Hickman?"

"Yes. Edwin had to sign some papers, and it's quicker to just come by so I can answer questions. Abby, I think we should have dinner and talk and reconsider not seeing each other socially. I have some questions to ask you. Now isn't the time or place because we can be interrupted at any moment. Can you go to dinner tomorrow night?"

"I still feel we need time and space and to see other people, and for now I want to stick with that. We're not in love, and we never have been. Maybe we're cheating ourselves out of a very good future. Let's leave it as is for now."

"I think you've let this Calhoun fellow influence you. He won't marry you, Abby. You should rethink some of your decisions, because you may be making a big mistake."

"I don't plan to marry him or want to. Right now I stand by my decision about us, and anyway, you're really busy with work."

"That's the truth. We'll talk this spring, but if you change your mind and want to go out, call me."

"Thanks, Lamont. I will. I need to relieve Justin," she added, starting toward the front. Lamont walked beside her. He would look at the problem from all angles he could think of and then draw his conclusion and tell her.

He sighed and shifted. "Perhaps you're right and we should go out with others for a while."

"I think it's a good idea," she said.

"Beckett single men don't ask you out because they know we date. Once they see me out with someone else, they'll start asking you out. Also, most everyone in town knows you've been to New York with a man from Dallas."

She smiled at him. "I'm not eager to go out with other men in town."

"Maybe not," he replied, looking distracted. "Abby, don't forget that I'm around if you want to talk. We're friends, no matter what."

"Yes, we are," she said, hurting and trying to be

careful what she said. "That's nice, Lamont, and I value your friendship." Impulsively, she brushed a light kiss on his cheek. "Go back to your work and we'll talk again later."

He looked at her for a long moment. "I guess I should have done more, maybe taken you less for granted."

"Don't blame yourself. I think this will be better for you, too."

"Perhaps," he said cautiously. "Take care." Lamont left her in the lobby as he went out the front door. In that moment, she was more certain than ever that she would never marry Lamont. Had she fallen in love with Josh so much that she would never love any other man? Was this a love for a lifetime? She thought of the old legend of kissing in the heart-shaped shadow. She had never really believed in it and still didn't, but in her life, it might come true. It wouldn't be true for Josh.

When her phone buzzed, she saw Josh was calling again. She still didn't want to talk yet. She hurt and if she talked to him, she felt he would realize her unhappiness. She didn't want him to. In a couple of hours, she would get back into her routine and be better able to handle talking to him.

Maybe she would get over him much sooner than she thought because she had just told him goodbye today. By the time a week passed, she might feel better about everything and able to think about telling Josh goodbye without any sadness.

Right now that didn't seem possible. He wanted to talk to her, so he must feel something—lust came to mind. He didn't feel anything else or he would never have asked her to live with him and travel with him.

Josh put away his phone. He couldn't concentrate on catching up on emails and text messages because

Abby wouldn't pick up. He had talked to Benny and knew she was back at the inn. No matter how busy she was, she would normally answer her phone, so the only reason for no answer had to be that she didn't want to talk to him.

Surprising himself, he already missed her. He had had various women in his life, affairs, some lasting longer than others, but he couldn't recall ever missing any woman the way he missed Abby. Even though he couldn't get her out of his mind, he had to because there was no future for them. She had made that clear before she boarded the plane. He wondered if she wanted marriage—somehow he suspected he might have gotten the same flat refusal if he had proposed marriage. It wouldn't have been with anger, though. She had been annoyed by being asked to move in with him.

He didn't know why it surprised her or why it angered her. Even if she didn't want to move in, she should have understood why he asked her. She should have been pleased that he liked her enough to ask. He never had understood Abby, and he still didn't. As simple as her life was, she was in many ways a mystery to him.

He needed to get his mind back on his business and forget her. Impatiently he pulled a stack of papers in front of him, looked at his calendar and swore. He picked up the first paper to read, forgetting about Abby.

She was out of his thoughts about fifteen minutes, until he recalled making love with her.

"Dammit, Abby," he whispered. How could she permeate his thoughts and life to such an extent? He could not have fallen in love, and Abby was definitely not the woman for him. She would never reciprocate any love from him except on a physical level, and she had ended that as swiftly as it had begun. "Dammit," he repeated in the empty office. He suspected she would not go out with him again, which was unique in his experience with women. It annoyed him now because he wanted to see her.

He shook his head. "Get a grip, Calhoun," he told himself. He should forget her and go on with life. They'd had a weekend. A month from now, it would be nothing except a dim memory. He was not in love with her. It would not do him any good if he was. He ran through the reasons again. He bent over papers on his desk to focus on work. Thirty minutes later, he realized he was staring into space, wondering whether Abby could work without thinking about him.

Nine

Abby's mother wanted to see her pictures from New York, so Abby copied all her photos to her laptop and then deleted from her phone the ones with Josh, leaving only the most obvious tourist pictures.

She headed next door and found her mom in the kitchen peeling potatoes for dinner. "Have a seat. Grandma is at her friend Imogene's house. Imogene's son came by and picked up your grandmother since she hasn't been able to get out for so long. She will be back in a couple of days."

Abby gave her mother a light squeeze around the waist. "Let me help you. You sit and I'll peel."

"No, I'm through and ready for a break," she said, dumping a bowl of peeled potatoes into a slow cooker that had the delicious aroma of a cooking roast.

"That smells so good. It makes me want to go back and change my menu for tonight," she said, watching her mother put a lid on the cooker, then wash and dry her hands.

"Did you have a good time in New York and at the ranch?"

"I had a wonderful time. I saw so many sights. I brought you something," she said, handing her mother a package wrapped in white paper and tied in blue ribbon.

"How nice. Let's get a cup of tea and sit while I open this."

"When she gets back, I have something for Grandma, too," Abby said.

Her mother opened her present and raised the lid on a box to find a sterling necklace. "Abby, it's beautiful. I love it. Thank you." She smiled at her daughter. "Now I want to hear about the trip and see pictures."

"I had a wonderful time," she said again. "I had a suite in the new hotel. Look at my pictures and I'll show you where I went." She spent the next hour talking to her mother about her trip. Finally she put away her phone and stood. "I'd better get back."

"You don't think you'll see Josh again?" her mother asked.

Abby shook her head. "No, there wasn't anything between us. He just asked me because I'd never been anywhere and he was going anyway. Also, as I told you, he asked because he was grateful to me for letting him stay at the B and B the night of the blizzard. I think this whole trip was a thank you for that," she said, trying to make light of Josh's attention.

Her mother studied her as they walked to the back door and stepped outside. "You really don't think you'll see him again?"

"No, I won't. It was just a special trip, Mom—what I said before, there isn't anything between us."

"I'm glad you had a good time, and I'm glad you're not in love with him, honey. I think that's for the best."

"I agree. I'll see you tomorrow. Thanks again for covering for me while I was gone."

She hurried back to the inn to take over the front desk. Josh had stopped calling, and she wasn't surprised. She didn't expect to hear any more from him.

In the late afternoon the first Friday in April, Abby looked at her reflection in the mirror. She wore navy slacks and a matching navy blouse. Her hair was parted and fell around her face. Her mother had covered the front while she had bought groceries, and she went to the front desk to relieve her mother.

No one was in the lobby. She heard a television and someone on the piano in the living room. She went to her room and pulled out her phone to look at the old, unreturned calls from Josh. She deleted all of them and sat browsing through the New York pictures on her phone. Josh wasn't in them, but she could see him in every one of them.

She didn't know about her future. Right now she just wanted to forget Josh Calhoun and go on with her life.

She would rather stay in her room and not have to talk to everyone, but she should relieve her mom, so she placed her phone in a dresser drawer and went to find her mother.

She found her in the living room and walked with her to the lobby. As her mother slipped into her coat, she said, "Josh Calhoun called you. I can see why you enjoyed going to New York with him."

"He's nice."

"He was very friendly, and we talked awhile. He told me he was sorry he didn't get to meet me and Grandma, because he'd heard a lot about us. He said it had been a lifesaver for you to let him stay during the blizzard."

"Josh can be charming, Mom. I won't deny that."

"He asked me to tell you that he called."

"Thanks. It's not important."

Her mother let out a long sigh as she frowned. "Abby, maybe I was wrong in being worried. Not all charming men are like your father. Don't be too influenced by the past. Josh seems to want to talk to you very much."

"Maybe, Mom, but I don't want to move in with him."

Her mother's brows arched. "If that's what he wants, then I'm glad you're not talking to him. That you don't need. Call me when you want me to cover again. If I can't, I'll tell you."

"Thanks, Mom," she said, kissing her mother's cheek as she hugged her lightly.

She followed her mother out and watched until she went inside next door. Then Abby went to her room. Tonight the guests would just have to be on their own or come get her because she didn't want to talk to anyone.

The phone extension rang in her room, and she picked it up. She talked with Colleen Grimes, her best friend, for a long time. It was a relief to tell Colleen a bit about Josh as well as breaking it off with Lamont. She was closer in some ways to Colleen than anyone else. Her sister was young, so her views of some things were not the same as Abby's, but she and Colleen had grown up knowing each other and had been best friends since first grade. They talked for almost an hour until she finally told Colleen goodbye.

She could hear her cell phone ringing in the drawer. She had heard it once when she talked to Colleen. After it stopped, she crossed the room to turn it off.

Her mother would call on the inn's phone if she needed her. Otherwise, Abby couldn't think of any call she would want to take.

That night she didn't sleep much but lay in the dark, recalling being in Josh's arms, kissing him, making love. She couldn't forget the fun and laughter they had shared. She wouldn't even think about traveling with him and what that life would be like, because it would never happen.

It was almost dawn when she fell into a restless sleep that was filled with dreams of Josh.

When she stirred in the morning, she felt groggy. She thought of her night and of Josh, wondering when he would stop calling and start forgetting her.

She spent the next week trying to immerse herself in work. Signs of spring finally began to appear even though late this year. With spring, their business picked up with guests who traveled once the weather improved.

Josh had stopped calling, and she wondered if he had already started seeing someone else. She guessed that he usually had a woman in his life. Some probably longer and more important than others. No matter how much she hurt thinking about him, she couldn't stop re-membering and wondering about him.

With the passing of another week, she didn't feel one degree less drawn to Josh. Actually, the hurt seemed to increase with each day instead of diminishing, but she still assumed that after a bit more time, it would fade until it was gone and he was an unimportant memory.

She hoped that's what would happen. Josh had stopped calling, so she assumed he was moving on with his life, and she felt certain he had stopped think-ing about her or wanting to see her. She expected to get over Josh eventually and just have the wonderful memories of New York.

She busied herself baking a cake and a pie for tomorrow. When she went to her room, she sat at her computer. She went through and wiped out all the pictures with Josh, which were already gone from her phone. As she did, she was unable to keep from crying. Josh was out of her life. Even if he wanted to see her again, she wouldn't because it would just mean more hurt, but she knew he was gone for good when his calls stopped.

In spite of keeping busy, she still couldn't keep Josh out of her thoughts. Who was he taking out this weekend?

It was the last Friday in April, and Josh struggled to pay attention to what was happening around him. He was in the executive meeting room at his brother Jake's Dallas office for a board of directors meeting.

Hands went up and he had no idea what he was voting on, but fortunately, it looked as if it would be unanimous. Even though he tried to focus on what was being said, in minutes his thoughts drifted to Abby. He wanted to see her again, and he couldn't understand why she wouldn't at least talk to him on the phone. What harm could that be?

His own actions puzzled him. He had never pursued a woman who obviously didn't want him in her life. Never before Abby. He just couldn't forget her.

The meeting was adjourned, and he remained in his seat. He was going to lunch with Jake. He didn't know who else from the board would go with them to eat, and he hoped he could pay more attention through lunch and get Abby out of his thoughts.

One by one, the others left the meeting room until the sole person left was Jake, who looked at him.

"We're the only ones going to lunch?" Josh asked.

"Yes. Everyone else had something to do."

Josh stood. "Okay. I'm ready to go. What's the deal with Mike? I never heard another thing from you about seeing him and Savannah when they return from their honeymoon."

"They're taking longer on their honeymoon because Scotty is doing fine and very happy staying with Lindsay. He loves his aunt Lindsay and doesn't want to leave. Then we'll keep him for a couple of nights, so Mike and Savannah are getting an extended honeymoon. I'll have a family dinner when they come back. The minute I have a possible date for the dinner, I'll send a text to everyone and let all of you know."

"Very good."

They left Jake's office building and walked down the street to the restaurant where they usually ate. After they had ordered hamburgers, Jake studied Josh. "Are you having business problems?"

"No. What makes you ask that? Things couldn't be going better—well, I guess they could be better, but they're plenty okay right now. No complaints. Financially, if the way this year has started is any indication, this is going to be a very good year."

"That's good to hear."

"Why the question?"

"You didn't know what was going on in that meeting today."

"Now, how do you know that?"

Jake shook his head. "I'm your brother, remember? I've known you a long time. I know when your thoughts are somewhere else, and they were really somewhere else—not much like you in a business meeting."

"Guess I was just thinking about a small chain of boutique hotels that has been presented to me at work as a good buy. My staff thinks I need to make a decision soon if I really want this. We don't usually deal with boutique hotels—it's a new concept to me. I just want to know what I'm getting into."

"I'd think your staff could handle that."

"They can, but I've been thinking about it. You had a good meeting today."

"I hate to say I'm going to profit out of marrying Madison, but so far, all indications are that her land is going to be lucrative for drilling."

"You don't know yet, but I'm glad it's looking that way."

"You never count on anything until it's absolutely signed, sealed and delivered and completely done," Jake said with a smile.

"It's paid off to be cautious. As for Madison, she'll be as happy as you are if you're right about her land. She knows that isn't why you married her."

"That's right." They ate in silence for a few minutes until Jake set down his water glass. "How was your trip to New York? I know you didn't go for a hotel opening."

Josh smiled. "No, I didn't, and it was fun."

"Ah, so are you seeing the B and B owner regularly now?"

"No, I'm not. It was fun and it's over. She isn't exactly my type, but she was nice and she'd never been anywhere, so I took her to New York."

Jake shook his head. "I'm not going to ask any more. I'd better get back to the office. Are you ready?"

"Yeah, I am, and I'll get the check this time."

"Okay, thanks," Jake said.

They walked back to Jake's office, where Josh told him goodbye, got in his car and drove to his office. He was busy the rest of the afternoon and finally drove home after five. He worked out, swam and ate leftovers even though there were casseroles in the refrigerator for him. A lot of the time he thought about Abby until he grabbed his phone and called one of the women he considered a good friend. He asked her out for the following night. The minute he finished the call, he regretted it because he didn't really want to go out with any woman except Abby.

The next night, when he picked Emma up, he tried to focus on her, but all he could do was think about Abby. Making another effort, he gazed at Emma Picket, a statuesque blonde, striking, between husbands at the moment. She was fun to be with, and occasionally he took her out. He hoped tonight she would take his mind off Abby. He thought of the brief relationship he'd had so long ago with Emma. It finally ended in a mutual agreement because she wanted to get married, so she moved on, but they stayed friends through her two marriages and divorces.

As she climbed into his car, his gaze swept over her dark blue sleeveless dress with a low V-neck that revealed a lush figure. She had long, shapely legs and he wondered why she wasn't out with a prospect for husband number three. In spite of her stunning looks, his pulse didn't speed or his breath catch. No response occurred that Abby could stir with her ponytail and no makeup. What was the magic Abby held that attracted him?

He took Emma to dinner, and they ate outside because the evening was perfect. She smiled at him and reached across the table to take his hand. "Now whom are you trying to get out of your life, or what knotty business problem do you have?"

"What makes you think I have a problem?"

"You look totally preoccupied, and you call me when you do."

He laughed and rubbed her soft hand, lifting it to his lips to brush a kiss across her knuckles. "You know me too well, but I know you just as well. Why are you out with me? Trying to forget husband number two or trying to make prospective husband number three jealous?"

She laughed. "Touché. The latter, Josh. And you?"

"You were right the first time," he said. "Trying to get someone out of my life, sort of," he added. He was trying to get her out of his thoughts.

"Ah." Emma glanced around the restaurant's patio at other couples. "Is she supposed to be here tonight and see us together?"

"No, I just wanted you to take my mind off her. She—" he paused "—worries me a little."

"Worries you? You never worry about a woman. Is she stalking you?"

"Oh, no."

Emma smiled. "Whatever's going on, I'm delighted because I didn't want to stay home tonight, and the man I need to make jealous eats here often enough that he might even show up. I've already said hello to two of his friends as we came in. Word should get back to him that I was here with you. Just excellent, Josh."

He smiled. "You make me feel better. When the dancing starts, we'll dance and I'll give them reason to tell him we were here together."

She laughed with him and her eyes sparkled. "Wonderful, darling."

Their waiter came and they ordered. Josh felt better because he could help Emma with her problem, and maybe his would diminish slightly. As he talked with Emma and their dinner came and they ate, his expectations of getting Abby out of his thoughts faded. He missed her, and even a good friend who was a fun person could not take his mind off her. He had the best time with Abby, and no one was going to get her out of his thoughts.

"Josh?" He realized Emma had said his name and was staring intently at him.

"I'm sorry. I had a business deal today that is hanging fire," he said to cover whatever made her stare at him.

"You haven't heard me. This isn't like you," she said, cocking her head to one side while she looked intently at him.

"Don't make too much of it. I'm just preoccupied."

Her eyes narrowed. "What's her name?"

"Whose name?" he asked.

"Josh, your mind is far away. You asked me out to help you forget someone." Her eyes widened and her mouth dropped open. "It's finally happened. You're the one who got left behind, and she walked out."

"Don't make a big deal of it, because it isn't a big deal."

"When did you break up?"

"Never. There was nothing to break up," he said, aware from Emma's expression that she didn't believe him.

"You're in love," she said, sounding shocked.

"No, I'm not in love," he said. "I've never told her I love her. I haven't known her long enough or well enough to be in love."

She laughed. "I never thought I would see the day.

You're so in love and you don't even know it." She giggled.

He stood. "C'mon, let's dance," he said, taking her hand.

On the dance floor, he held her close. She was soft, voluptuous, her perfume enticing, and she simply made him miss Abby more than ever. What kind of spell had Abby woven? Maybe he had tempted fate when he kissed her in the shadow caused by the full moon. That was a better explanation than any other he could come up with.

He had wanted Emma to make him forget Abby, but that wasn't going to happen. But in spite of his dilemma, he could help Emma. "Are the friends still here?"

"Oh, yes. I just smiled at one of them."

Josh dipped low, and her hands tightened on his shoulders as she clung to him. He swung her up and kissed her, wanting her to kiss him and make him forget everything else, to put an end to this constant need to want to be with Abby.

Instead, he just wanted Abby in his arms. He wanted to kiss her. Emma's kiss was meaningless and did nothing to stir him. He released her to continue dancing, but he wanted the evening to end so he could take Emma home.

"I have a long day tomorrow," he said. "I'll take you home."

"That's fine, but you don't have to lie about the long day. You're trying to get over someone, and I didn't help." She patted his hand. "I have no doubt you'll get over her eventually, but Josh, this was bound to happen at some point in your charmed life. She must be quite a woman."

"Emma, don't—"

"Shh. Don't worry. I understand, and since you've never been through this, it has probably hit you like a meteorite zooming to your little patch of earth. You'll live, Josh. Maybe you'll even have to think about marriage. If you do," she said, laughter in her voice, "please be sure to send me an invitation to the wedding, because I want to meet her."

He took Emma home and for a moment they sat in his car. "You're just blowing this all out of proportion."

"I don't think so." She kissed his cheek. "I definitely think you're in love, and you never have been in your life, so you can't even recognize the signs. I had a good time, had a good dinner and accomplished my purpose tonight. I'm sorry I couldn't make you forget her, but if you're in love, no one and nothing short of a total disaster will make you forget her. Knowing you, you'll win over your fair maiden. She must really be something to tie you in knots."

"She is, Emma," he said, thinking he could see Emma as a beautiful woman, a friend, but nothing more. Abby dazzled him, took his breath, and he couldn't ever view her in an ordinary way.

Emma looked intently at him and patted him on the shoulder. "You're really in love. Don't forget to invite me to the wedding."

He got out of the car and opened her door for her. "Don't hold your breath. She won't even answer my phone calls. I'm not her type."

Emma looked as if she might be biting her lip as Josh walked her to her front door. She turned to face him and once again was composed as she smiled. "Thanks for tonight."

"You're a real friend, Emma. Good luck with your latest guy. I hope he's a good one. You deserve it."

"Thanks." She blew him a kiss as she stepped farther inside and closed her door.

He walked back to his car, already forgetting Emma and thinking about Abby. Was he in love and didn't even know it? He didn't think such a thing was possible. Should he look at engagement rings? The notion was so foreign to him, he shook his head. They didn't know each other well enough to get married. She would reject that as swiftly as she had his proposition.

If she wouldn't answer his calls, the only thing he could think to do was to go see her. He had to get her out of his system, but at the moment he wanted some more time with her. If an affair with her was impossible, he'd just take her out. He thought about getting her a gift and vetoed it. Abby had some very old-fashioned and strong ideas about what she thought appropriate and wanted and what she didn't. How in hell had he gotten attracted to her?

As swiftly as the question came, the answer came— he had the best time with her he had ever had with any woman. How could he have ruined that wonderful weekend so completely that she wouldn't even talk to him? He knew exactly how, and he wished he had given more thought to asking her to move in with him.

He focused on going to see her. He wished he had met her mother and made friends with her. Instead, he called Edwin Hickman. He needed to find out when he could catch Abby where she had to talk to him and wouldn't slam a door in his face.

His usual self-assurance with a woman was leaving him fast. He was lost with Abby, unable to figure her out and hoping he would do the right thing. If this failed, he didn't see any hope of another chance.

He thought about his situation all the way to his

house. Once inside, he sat in a darkened bedroom that had light only from the hall, staring into space, still lost in thought.

He thought about Emma laughing at him. Was he in love with Abby? Really in love? If he was, he sure as hell hadn't followed logic in falling in love. Abby didn't like his lifestyle—there were a million problems. He raked his fingers through his hair. Did he love her? Really love her in a lifetime-with-someone kind of way? And even if he did, how could he ever get her to accept a marriage proposal since she didn't like his lifestyle, didn't trust him to ever settle and didn't want a husband who traveled? He had to think this through before he botched it.

"Dammit to hell, Abby." That night of the blizzard he should have gone home with Benny and slept on the floor with the in-laws and the kids and the baby. He wasn't ready for marriage. He wasn't ready to lose Abby, either. And if he proposed marriage, she would turn him down. That thought tied him in knots.

For the first time in his life, he was in love, and she didn't love him back. And she had enough backbone, no matter how irresistible she found him physically, to resist him totally.

A lifetime with Abby—right now that looked like a really good future, but an impossible one. He couldn't even get her to talk to him. How would he get her to marry him?

He had to admit that he must be in love. He would have laughed at himself and the situation if he hadn't hurt so badly. His brothers and Lindsay would laugh at him and probably say he deserved this. Maybe Mike wouldn't, since he'd fallen in love recently, but Jake and Lindsay would.

He was in love with Abby, and he hadn't even known the extent of his feelings for her until everything blew up in his face. He wanted to get her an engagement ring, something old-fashioned and sentimental, if diamonds could ever be old-fashioned and sentimental.

He needed to start figuring out what he would have to do to convince her to marry him. She wasn't even talking to him. It seemed the most daunting task he had ever faced. He got up and went to his desk to switch on a light. He grabbed a sheet of paper and jotted down the arguments she would throw at him for reasons she could not marry him. He numbered them, writing carefully and then staring into space, thinking about all the things she had said to him.

The moment the decision was made, he started planning. He felt better except that for the first time in his life, he had a running current of worry that she wouldn't even talk to him in person and give him a chance to propose.

Ten

Abby had just checked in two guests, and Justin was helping so she didn't have to show the couple to their room. She left the desk. Glancing at the clock, she saw it was almost seven.

"Ah, Abby," Mr. Hickman said, coming into the lobby. "It is a lovely evening, and I hope I can interest you in sitting with me on the front porch."

She smiled and linked her arm with his. "Of course you can. I would love to sit in the swing and do nothing but talk to you and enjoy the evening. It's hard to believe that recently we had snow."

"That was a freak, late snowstorm, although they do happen. Mother Nature is trying to make up for it tonight."

Mr. Hickman sat in a rocker. Abby sat on the porch swing and began to swing slowly. "This is wonderful," she said. "There is something soothing about a porch swing."

SARA ORWIG   173

"I hope you are feeling patient, my dear. Your friend called me and is coming to see you."

Startled, she turned to look at him. Just then a car entered the parking lot at the side of the front yard. She watched the black sports car whip into a space. When Josh stepped out, her heart thudded. He wore his white Stetson, a white dress shirt open at the throat, jeans and his boots, and he looked even more breathtaking to her than before. She curbed an impulse to run and throw herself into his arms. Instead, she sat very still, certain this visit would be a deeper hurt.

"Here he is, Mr. Hickman."

"Yes, indeed. You're so kind to me, Abby. Be kind to him tonight."

Not trusting herself to speak, she nodded. If she hadn't been hurting so badly, she would have laughed over Mr. Hickman's ridiculous request.

She wasn't even aware when Mr. Hickman left. Her heart pounded and a mixture of feelings tore at her, but excitement dominated. As Josh bounded to the porch, he looked filled with vitality.

She reminded herself that whatever he wanted to do, she had to say no. She couldn't go out with him again. She definitely would not take a trip again with him.

She clamped her mouth closed and clenched her fists, jamming them into her pockets to hide them. She wished she had changed. She had on the same pink knit shirt and jeans she had put on when she got up this morning. Her hair probably needed to be combed and her ponytail redone. She shouldn't even care, but she felt self-conscious in spite of knowing she should send him on his way.

When he walked up to her to stand close, her heart pounded.

"Hi. I saw Edwin when I turned into the lot, so he must have told you I called him."

"Yes. Until then I didn't know you were coming."

"You wouldn't answer your phone."

"No, we really don't have anything more to say to each other. I don't know why you came all the way to Beckett."

"I want to talk to you. Can we go to your suite?"

She started to say no, looked into his dark eyes and nodded in spite of wary feelings.

"Good. You won't be sorry," he said with his usual take-charge self-assurance.

Holding the door for her, he walked beside her. Intensely aware of him so close, she felt their shoulders lightly brush as they walked, and a tingle slithered down her arm from the faintest contact. In her suite, she closed the door behind her.

"Would you like to sit?" she asked.

"If you will," he said. She moved to a wingback chair so he couldn't sit beside her.

He pulled another chair close. "I've missed you, and I wanted to talk to you. Abby, I shouldn't have asked you to move in with me or travel with me."

"No, you shouldn't have. You know I'm old-fashioned, tied to the B and B, very close to my family. Under those circumstances, your invitation indicated to me that you really don't know me and you don't care a lot about me. I understand that part, Josh. I never expected you to fall in love. Frankly, I never expected to, either."

"I should have thought that one through, and I didn't. It was a spur-of-the-moment impulse because I didn't want to tell you goodbye or have you fly out of my life. I've thought things through this time, and I have definitely fallen in love with you."

His words stunned her, and her heart thudded.

Standing, he stepped in front of her, took her hand and knelt on one knee. "Abby, I love you."

With those four words, her heart began to pound as she stared at him in shock.

"Will you marry me?"

"Josh—" she whispered, even more stunned and barely able to get her breath or voice. He held up a hand as if motioning her to wait.

She wanted to stop him, yet she couldn't. She had never thought about the possibility of a marriage proposal. *I love you.* The words echoed in her mind. "You can't love me," she said, barely able to get out the words. "You don't know me that well."

"Yes, I do love you. We had that weekend. We've worked together, laughed together, danced, kissed, made love. I just know that I don't want to go through life without you," he said. "Please listen," he added quickly. "I've thought about this. You object to several things about my lifestyle, my traveling and my cosmopolitan life. I can change that. I can turn my business over to very competent people and retire now to the ranch. I have enough money that I don't need to step into my office ever again if I don't want to."

As he talked, her heart raced. She had turned to ice, but now she warmed. Feeling dazed, she listened to him while all she could think was that he loved her and he indicated he would change his life for her.

"Josh, I'm shocked. I can't believe you mean this or know what you're doing."

"I usually do know what I'm doing, and I'm sure I know this time. It's been hell without you in my life. Abby, marry me. I love you," he said.

Her heart pounded. "You would move to the ranch permanently?"

"Yes, whatever you want. You don't know how I love you. I'll be happy on the ranch. I was going to live there anyway. This way, I'm just moving there sooner, and I'd have you with me."

"Josh, you're not thinking. I have this bed-and-breakfast. I can't just walk out and leave the inn."

"No, you can't. I can buy it from you and run it just as it is. You can pay off your mother's house with the money and pay for your siblings to finish college. I have enough money that we can do whatever you want to do. If your family wants to be closer, I can move them to Verity. Abby, we can do whatever we want about your family." His dark eyes were intent on her, and his voice was filled with conviction. She felt stunned, amazed as she listened.

"I have enough money to take care of all of them, aunts included. We'll take care of Edwin, too. He won't be moved out. It's just no problem. If they want to stay here, I have family planes at my disposal, and you can fly back and forth. The problem is, I don't want to go through life without you."

She felt dizzy as she looked at him and tried to fathom what he was telling her.

"Josh, you've had a lot of women in your life. I can't see you settling down."

He stood and pulled her to her feet to wrap his arms around her. She placed her hands on his forearms.

"I love you with all my heart," he declared. "I want to live on the ranch with you or wherever you'd like to live. I want you with me, Abby. That's what's important. Will you marry me?"

"I just can't believe you really are in love and won't change your mind."

"I promise. I won't change my mind."

"I don't even know if you want children."

"Yes, I do," he said. "Abby, for heaven's sake, you're doing me in here— don't tell me you haven't missed me or thought about me."

Her heart pounded. Josh was in love with her. He wanted to marry her, and he would move to his ranch and take care of the inn. Lost in thought about all he had said, she stared at him another minute while all color drained from his face.

"Abby, I want to marry you," he repeated.

Hoping he meant every word, she threw her arms around his neck. "I guess you have to take chances in life. I love you, Josh." She stood on tiptoe to kiss him. It took one startled second before his arms tightened around her and he kissed her in return, a hard, possessive kiss that reaffirmed his declaration of love.

Suddenly she leaned back to look at him. "I haven't met your family. You don't know Mom or my grandmother."

"So we'll meet everybody. It'll work out."

"Suppose your family doesn't like me?"

"That's totally impossible," he said, kissing her again. He finally raised his head. "Abby, give me an answer—"

"Yes, I'll marry you. I love you with all my heart."

He kissed again, passionately, a long kiss that made her heart pound with joy and all doubts crumble and fade.

"We need to tell our families," Josh said when he released her. "Can I have a room for the night?"

She laughed. "Yes, you can stay in a room or on my

sofa. That's your choice. You don't get any other choice, because I don't have privacy here."

"I'll settle for whatever I can get. Oh, wait. I'm not doing this right," he said, reaching in his pocket to pull out a box. Another shock rocked her when she saw his hands shake. He fumbled trying to get the top off the box until she had to hold back a smile. He yanked off the top and tossed it to the floor, taking out a smaller black box, which he opened. "If this doesn't fit or you don't like it, we can change it," he said.

She stared at a huge, dazzling diamond. "Josh, that is so beautiful," she said.

He removed it from the box and dropped the box to take her hand and slip the ring on her finger.

"It's heart-shaped," she said.

"That's so you'll remember the night we kissed in the heart-shaped shadow," he said. "We'll work everything out, I promise."

She looked up, and his dark eyes were filled with love. "Josh," she whispered, throwing her arms around him tightly as she kissed him. "I love you."

He crushed her against him, kissing her possessively.

Finally he released her. "I can't ever express how much I've missed you. Let's go tell your relatives and then we'll call my family. We're planning a family dinner soon, so you can meet all of them."

She framed his face with her hands. "You're sure about giving up your business? That's an enormous life change. Maybe I can make some concessions."

"I'm sure. I love ranching, and I don't want to travel and be away from you. I'll see more of all my family, which is a plus. Think you can live in the boonies on a ranch?"

She laughed and waved her hand at her surroundings. "What do you think? Of course, I can. Look at the life I lead now."

"You always have people around you. You won't have a bunch at the ranch."

"Maybe we can work on that one," she said, smiling at him as she kissed him again.

After a few minutes, he raised his head. "We're engaged. You're sure I go on the sofa tonight?"

"On the sofa or in another room."

"Let's set this wedding date soon. The Colorado trip may have to be postponed slightly. I'll still go, just a little later."

"Mr. Hickman will understand."

She gazed into Josh's brown eyes, and her heart beat faster because love filled his expression. He had never looked at her the way he did now, with warmth and intense longing. He drew her close to kiss her once more, a long kiss that made her heart pound. When he raised his head to look at her, he touched her cheek, caressing her lightly with his fingertips. "I've been through hell without you."

"I've missed you, too," she whispered, certain she would remember this night for the rest of her life, even though at the moment it held a dreamlike quality.

He took her hand. "Who do we tell first?"

"If I get my choice, I'd say let's tell my mom right away. Let me call and see if she's home. She'll be happy, Josh." In minutes she put away her phone. "She said to come over."

"I want to get moving so we can start planning a wedding."

As they walked to her mother's house, Josh's cell phone rang and he answered. He took her wrist to stop her and put his phone on speaker. "This is my brother Jake. I'm going to tell him now."

She nodded and listened. "Jake, I have this on speaker. I'm with Abby Donovan."

"Hi, Abby Donovan," Jake said.

She smiled as Josh put his arm around her shoulders. "Jake, I was going to call you. You go first though."

"Mike and Savannah came home. We're having dinner a week from Friday night."

"I'll clear my calendar," Josh answered. "I'm bringing Abby." He looked at her.

"Abby, you're definitely invited," Jake said.

"Thank you. That date is fine with me," she said, looking at Josh.

"It'll be fun, and Abby can meet the family and vice versa."

"Look forward to it. Now what are you calling me about?"

"Jake, I've asked Abby to marry me, and she's accepted. We're engaged," Josh announced, smiling at Abby and kissing her briefly.

"Congratulations to you. Abby, we're delighted to have you in the family and look forward to meeting you. That's wonderful news."

"Thank you," she said, smiling. "I'm happy and I can't wait to meet Josh's family."

"I'll call the others tonight," Josh added. "You're the first person we've told."

"That's really good news, Josh. I'm glad."

"I'll talk to you later," Josh said. "We're on our way to tell Abby's mom and grandmom."

"Have fun. Talk to you, bro."

The call ended, and after giving Abby a hug, Josh dropped the phone into his pocket.

They reached her mother's house. Abby went ahead, calling to her mother, who appeared and ushered them into the kitchen.

"Mom, I want you to meet Josh Calhoun. Josh, this is my mother, Nell Donovan."

"I'm glad to meet you," Nell said. "Now I have a chance to thank you for clearing snow off my driveway."

"I was glad to do it, and I'm glad to meet you."

"Mom, Josh has asked me to marry him. We're engaged," she said, holding out her hand for her mother to see her ring.

"Oh, Abby, how marvelous," Nell said, hugging her daughter and turning to Josh. "Welcome to our family, Josh. Justin will be thrilled to have another male in the family." She looked at the ring. "What a gorgeous ring. That's breathtaking."

"Mrs. Donovan, I know it's old-fashioned, but since Abby's father is gone, maybe I should have asked your permission first."

"If you make Abby happy, you have my permission. I think this is wonderful. We need to tell Grandma. You know what she will worry about, but we'll work it out."

"Josh already has, Mom. Let's go tell Grandma and sit and let Josh tell you what he has offered." Abby smiled at him and linked her arm through his. "Come meet my grandmother. We both have a lot of relatives to meet."

"Arden is on her way here to pick up something. When you tell her, they'll probably hear her screaming with joy at the inn," her mother remarked. "She'll think this is very romantic."

"Mom's right. Hold your ears, Josh, when we tell her."

They all laughed as they went to the living room

to find her grandmother. Abby wanted to shout with
joy herself, and she kept glancing at the ring that was
merely a symbol of what she and Josh had found in
each other.

Butterflies were in her stomach as she stood in the
foyer with the wedding planner and Justin at her side.
She couldn't believe the date had finally arrived—a
Saturday morning, the fourth weekend in May. Arden
was maid of honor, and her best friend, Colleen, and
Josh's sister, Lindsay, were bridesmaids. They all wore
ankle-length yellow silk crepe dresses with spaghetti
straps and straight skirts.

Abby glanced briefly at the groomsmen: Josh's
brother Jake was best man, and Mike and two of
Josh's friends from college were groomsmen. When
she looked at Josh, all her nervous jitters ceased. He
was so handsome it took her breath away, and she still
couldn't believe she was about to become his wife and
move to his ranch. He had already bought the bed-and-
breakfast, hired someone to run it and made arrangements to pay Arden's and Justin's college costs. He'd
paid off her mother's house. He had flown all her family, including her aunts and Mr. Hickman, to Dallas,
and they were staying at a large hotel owned by Josh.

Right now, all she wanted was to be with Josh and
leave for their honeymoon.

Justin took her arm. "You look pretty, sis," he said
quietly, and she smiled at him.

"Thank you. You look quite handsome yourself," she
said, thinking he did look handsome in his black tux.

"I think all of Beckett has turned out for the wedding, including Lamont," he said. "I can't think of anyone we know who isn't here."

"I noticed, and I'm amazed they all came. Mom is friends with a lot of people."

"I believe you are, too," he said.

"It's time," the wedding planner stated. With a nod at Justin, they stepped off together to start down the aisle. Again, she could see only Josh.

She went through the ceremony in a daze, looking at the slim gold wedding band that held a row of diamonds.

Then they were introduced to the guests as Mr. and Mrs. Josh Calhoun. Josh kissed her briefly, smiling at her as he linked her arm in his to leave.

Later, at the reception at a Dallas club, Josh took her hand for the first dance. When the band began to play a Strauss waltz, she smiled at him. "You did this and didn't tell me."

"I did. I thought you'd want a waltz."

"I love it," she said. "And you waltz divinely."

"I don't know about that. No one's ever said that to me before, but great," he said, laughing. "Soon my dad will dance with you. My mom thinks you're wonderful and a very good influence on me."

Abby laughed. "I hope I'm a good influence and not a bad one."

"Never. My brothers will dance with you, too."

"Your sister has been so nice to me. They all are. You have a very nice family. There are also a lot of Milans here. I think that feud is dead."

"You're new to the family. It's not dead because Tony and Lindsay keep it going. If you'll notice, they stay on opposite sides of the room. He's a friend, so I put him on the wedding list, but he won't stay at this reception, and the sole reason he'll leave is Lindsay. The feud isn't over yet."

"Well, you still have a very nice family. All the Calhouns have been friendly and welcoming. They've been that way to my family, too."

"Thanks. They're glad to have you join the family. Everyone thinks you'll be good for me," he said, grinning.

"Maybe it's best I don't know a whole lot about your life."

"I'll tell you most anything you want to know."

"I'm quite happy with what I know now," she said. "Lamont will probably dance with me, and I'm sure you don't mind."

"Not at all."

"I hope Lamont finds someone who is really in love with him."

"He probably will now that you're out of the way. See the blonde standing at the edge of the dance floor and talking to three guys?"

"Yes. She came through the receiving line. Emma, I think."

He nodded. "She's an old, close friend. I took her out to try to get you out of my system when I came back from Beckett. She figured out before we got through dinner that I was in love with someone else and thought it very funny that I had finally fallen in love. She asked me to invite her to the wedding."

"She may be a close friend, but she's not old. She's stunning."

"Definitely not as stunning as my bride. When I was out with her, all I did was think about you and miss you. You're gorgeous, Abby, and you've made me the happiest man on earth today."

"I hope so. I love you, Josh. I love my beautiful heart ring. See, I told you that night you were tempting fate

by following that old legend of kissing in the shadow.
Once again it came true."

"I'm damn glad I did tempt fate," he said, smiling
at her.

"We'll be leaving soon, and you said you would surprise me with the honeymoon you've planned. I think
it's time to tell me."

"We fly to New York and then to Vienna, where you
can waltz your way through this honeymoon."

"Josh, I'm thrilled. Thrilled with Vienna and the
waltz prospects."

"We'll also go to Switzerland and Germany so you
can see all the castles you want."

"I feel as if I'm dreaming."

"I do, too," he said, suddenly looking at her intently
and losing his smile. "I love you more than I can show
you, but I'm going to try every day of my life."

"Don't make promises you can't keep."

"I intend to keep that promise, Abby. I mean it. I
need you more than you'll ever know."

"There are some things about you I'll never understand. You shouldn't have had a shred of interest in me."

"I told you to remember the old saying, 'opposites
attract,' and believe me, you attracted me from the first
moment I looked into your big, blue eyes."

She smiled. "I could say the same in reverse. I'll be
glad when we can leave."

"Just let me know when. I was ready when we walked
down the aisle."

It was eight that evening when he carried her into
the penthouse at his New York hotel. He set her on her
feet and looked at her a moment in a silent exchange, his
dark eyes filled with love. Wrapping his arms around

her, he kissed her. Abby clung to him, kissing him passionately, letting her love pour through. Happiness filled her. She was starting life with Josh, the only man she had ever really loved.

* * * * *

If you loved this novel, read more in the
LONE STAR LEGENDS *series from*
USA TODAY *bestselling author Sara Orwig*

THE TEXAN'S FORBIDDEN FIANCÉE
A TEXAN IN HER BED
AT THE RANCHER'S REQUEST

Available now from Harlequin Desire!

If you're on Twitter, tell us what you think of
Harlequin Desire! #harlequindesire

COMING NEXT MONTH FROM

◆ HARLEQUIN®

Desire

Available June 2, 2015

#2377 WHAT THE PRINCE WANTS
Billionaires and Babies • by Jules Bennett
Needing time to heal, a widowed prince goes incognito. He hires a
live-in nanny for his infant daughter but soon finds he wants the woman
for *himself*. Is he willing to cross the line from professional to personal?

#2378 CARRYING A KING'S CHILD
Dynasties: The Montoros • by Katherine Garbera
Torn between running his family's billion-dollar shipping business
and assuming his ancestral throne, Rafe Montoro needs to let off
some steam. But his night with a bartending beauty could change
everything—because now there's a baby on the way...

#2379 PURSUED BY THE RICH RANCHER
Diamonds in the Rough • by Catherine Mann
Driven by his grandmother's dying wish, a Texas rancher must choose
between his legacy and the sexy single mother who unknowingly holds
the fate of his heart—and his inheritance—in her hands.

#2380 THE SHEIKH'S SECRET HEIR
by Kristi Gold
Billionaire Tarek Azzmar knows a secret that will destroy the royal family
who shunned him. But the tables turn when he learns his lover is near
and dear to the royal family *and* she's pregnant with his child.

#2381 THE WIFE HE COULDN'T FORGET
by Yvonne Lindsay
Olivia Jackson steals a second chance with her estranged husband
when he loses his memories of the past two years. But when he finally
remembers *everything*, will their reconciliation stand the ultimate test?

#2382 SEDUCED BY THE CEO
Chicago Sons • by Barbara Dunlop
When businessman Riley Ellis learns that his rival's wife has a secret
twin sister, he seduces the beauty as leverage and then hires her to
keep her close. But now he's trapped by his own lies...and his desires...

REQUEST YOUR FREE BOOKS!
2 FREE NOVELS PLUS 2 FREE GIFTS!

H HARLEQUIN®

Desire

ALWAYS POWERFUL, PASSIONATE AND PROVOCATIVE

*Will Rafe Montoro have to choose between the throne
and newfound fatherhood?*

*Read on for a sneak preview of
CARRYING A KING'S CHILD,
a DYNASTIES: THE MONTOROS novel
by USA TODAY bestselling author
Katherine Garbera.*

Pregnant!

He knew Emily wouldn't be standing in his penthouse apartment telling him this if he wasn't the father. His first reaction was joy.

A child.

It wasn't something he'd ever thought he wanted, but the idea that Emily was carrying his baby seemed right to him.

Maybe that was just because it gave him something other than his royal duties to think about. He'd been dreading his trip to Alma. He was flattered that the country that had once driven his family out had come back to them, asked them—him, as it turned out—to be the next king. But he had grown up here in Miami. He didn't want to be a stuffy royal.

He didn't want European paparazzi following him around and trying to catch him doing anything that would bring shame to his family. Including having a child out of wedlock.

"Rafe, did you hear what I said?"

"Yeah, I did. Are you sure?" he asked at last.

She gave him a fiery look from those aqua-blue eyes of hers. He'd seen the passionate side of her nature, and he guessed he was about to witness her temper. Hurricane Em was about to unleash all of her fury on him, and he didn't blame her one bit.

He held his hand up. "Slow down, Red. I didn't mean are you sure it's mine. I meant…are you sure you're pregnant?"

"Damned straight. And I wouldn't be here if I wasn't sure it was yours. Listen, I don't want anything from you. I know you can't turn your back on your family and marry me, and frankly, we only had one weekend together, so I'd have to say no to a proposal anyway. But…I don't want this kid to grow up without knowing you."

"Me neither."

She glanced up, surprised.

He'd sort of surprised himself. But it didn't seem right for a kid of his to grow up without him. He wanted that. He wanted a chance to impart the Montoro legacy…not the one newly sprung on him involving a throne, but the one he'd carved for himself in business. "Don't look shocked."

"You've kind of got a lot going on right now. And having a kid with me isn't going to go over well."

"Tough," he said. "I still make my own decisions."

Available June 2015 wherever
Harlequin® Desire books and ebooks are sold.

www.Harlequin.com

THE WORLD IS BETTER WITH

Romance

Harlequin has everything from contemporary, passionate and heartwarming to suspenseful and inspirational stories.

Whatever your mood, we have a romance just for you!

Connect with us to find your next great read, special offers and more.

f /HarlequinBooks

🐦 @HarlequinBooks

www.HarlequinBlog.com

www.Harlequin.com/Newsletters

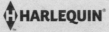

◆H HARLEQUIN®

A *Romance* FOR EVERY MOOD™

www.Harlequin.com